Meta

MW00717286

By Richard Vollmer

Table of Contents

Prologue – Echelon

Echelon was the last habitable world to be discovered before the start of the civil war and saw limited fighting during the near-decade of conflict. In the final deal between Earth and Novus, the world came to be jointly controlled. It wasn't until post-war that legitimate scientific and colonization efforts were launched, and competition to gain ground on-world was fierce. However, as other priorities surfaced, combined with the massive expenses involved in such far-off colonization, both empires abandoned the effort. Over time, the world became an unusual blend of Terran and Novian cultures and a jump-off point for expeditions further into the galaxy. Despite a lack of significant support from the larger empires, the world had also established itself as a blooming economic power. This, combined with newly discovered resources in the area, led to renewed interest in the sector, prompting both Earth and Novus to take a second look.

Chapter 1 - News

28 August 2431 – 01:22

Police Chief Eckhart watched as his two Lieutenants filed in. One was clearly anxious while the other bore a more serious expression.

"Close the door, sit down."

A moment later, the door was shut, and they were both seated. The Chief then scanned the glass wall behind them before proceeding.

"I assume that you have heard the rumors, gentlemen?"

Both nodded.

"We are to continue operating as normal until we receive more concrete information. As of now, this could just be some sort of mix up."

Both nodded, then the anxious one spoke up. "Should we not be preparing our personnel just in case? If that transmission was legitimate-"

"No. Your men are to continue operating normally. No changes to our shifts, no changes to our patrols. None of this leaves the room."

Now the more serious one spoke up. "What do you want us to do?"

"Stay awake and keep your ears open. I've arranged a meeting with a representative from our armed forces. We'll be meeting tomorrow morning to discuss what role our department is to take up."

"So, we are preparing?"

"No." The Chief stared at the Lieutenant. "The information we have is insufficient to act on."

"Right."

Hearing footsteps down the hallway, they all stopped talking. A few seconds later, the footsteps faded.

"One of your men has an orbital monitor, correct?" asked Eckhart, turning to the anxious Lieutenant.

"Yes. Yes, sir."

"Call him into work today, make sure he is not using it. When his shift ends, take him out for drinks, anything. Just keep him away from it."

"Yeah," he replied meekly.

The Chief rapped his knuckles on his desk. "Again, gentlemen, no one receives this information. I expect you both at the meeting tomorrow. Hopefully, we'll have more to work with then." He stared at them for one more second. Both were hoping for something more conclusive. "You're both dismissed. Go home, get a good night's sleep. You will need it."

At this, both stood up, saluted, and exited the room, closing the door behind them. Eckhart looked down at the papers on his desk. They seemed so trivial now. Finally, he decided that he should take his own advice and go home. Opening the top drawer of his desk, he pulled out a compact handgun. After checking that it was loaded, he slipped it into his pocket. Standing up, he turned off his office lights and stepped out.

Chapter 2 - Introductions

28 August 2431 – 10:02

Captain Honig of the Earth Union Civil Enforcement Office stepped out of the coffee shop, mug in hand. He was of average height, with a thin frame and grey hair. Despite his age, he maintained a bolt-upright posture. Overall, it was a genuinely nice day. It was less humid than usual, and the air was cool. The usual breeze had slowed to a minimum, indicative of the slow beginning of winter here. He took a sip of the hot liquid. Coffee here was a watered-down beverage of sorts, created with a synthetic powder meant to imitate coffee beans. Despite its shortcomings in flavor, it made up for it with the desired effects. Honig seldom had "real" coffee, and he considered it to be too strong a beverage.

From here, the sides of the valley could not be seen, being blocked out by rows of uniformly two-story buildings. It would have been a pretty view. The trees of this world were jet black in color and grew thickly in the flatlands at the bottom and tops of the valley. The steeper sides were covered in a dark green tallgrass-like plant, which proved to be resilient to all but the most determined clearing efforts. Neither the trees nor the grass here were particularly sensitive to wind either, so they stood still in all but the strongest gusts. Combined with the consistently silver-colored sky, it made for a genuinely surreal experience for off-worlders.

Slowly, Honig stepped up to the armored monstrosity that was his patrol vehicle, an aging black and white TAV-26 main battle tank that the department had procured through some surplus program. The cost of getting it here from Earth must have been astronomical, especially for its eventual use as just another patrol car. The department treated it as his vehicle. Honig was one of only two individuals who could operate it proficiently, and the other guy had elected to take up a desk job proceeding his retirement. Though completely impractical for its current use, the powers that be had decided that it was necessary to have considering the "particularly heated politics of the region." Perhaps they were heated on far off worlds like Earth or Novus, but no one cared here on Echelon.

"You all set, Frank?"

Honig looked up at Specialist Hershall, who was sitting on the main gun of the beast. He was young for this department, likely in his early twenties and sporting the clear, pale complexion typical of people on Echelon.

"Yeah, give me a minute." Honig placed his mug on the tank's fender and stretched his stiff knees briefly. At 78 years of age, he was really too old for this. A variety of high-cost augmentations and no will to retire, on the other hand, made him able to. Hershall helped pull him up, and soon Honig had lowered himself into the commander's hatch, mug in hand. Inside the turret, Officer Shepard sat asleep in the loader's position, his back against the turret's left wall. He was edging on heavyset and somehow managed to maintain an indefinite suntan despite a general lack of sun exposure. His standard-issue light infantry armor, characteristic of Earth Union police, rendered him near unable to fit in here. The uncomfortable appearance of his current position was borderline comical.

"Rise and shine!"

Shepard awoke with a start. "People these days, no respect." He rubbed his eyes.

Honig laughed. Activating the internal comms, he told Hershall that they were all set, and the vehicle shuttered as they started moving forward. Today was their usual patrol route: a quick trip through the housing district, then back north to the industrial district's southern edge. By the time they finished, they'd have just enough time before the end of shift to refuel and return to the station. At this point, the patrols were more for keeping the tank up and running than actual law enforcement.

The majority of the city's population was still composed of scientific personnel and support staff - the original settlers. It was always interesting seeing new families move in. Unlike the scientists, they tended to be less focused on utility. Thus, slowly but surely, they brought more color to the rows of prefabricated metal structures that composed the housing districts. The civilian population here was brand new and screened heavily before being allowed to come to Echelon, so crime wasn't really a thing. Even with populations from two competing empires, the mutual distrust that was prominent among the upper levels of governments was nearly non-existent among the civilian populous, even among the two police departments here.

All three of the tank's hatches were open so that its crew could be seen as they turned onto Mainstreet. In most cities, the massive, slow-moving hulk of metal would be an inconvenience, but there were still very few automobiles on-world. As of now, most vehicles were public transportation, and even those were scarce. A quarter of a kilometer down the road, they spotted a Novus Public Protection patrol car parked on the sidewalk, its two officers leaning against its side and conversing with someone. As Honig and his crew approached, they revved the engines filling the street with a cloud of white exhaust. One of the Novian officers responded by throwing an empty soda can that bounced off the tank's turret.

"Remember to be professional and courteous!" shouted Shepard. It was the Novus Police Corps' slogan.

"Don't make me write you a citation for reckless driving!" one of them shouted back, laughing.

"And I'll get you for littering!" Shepard replied, his voice nearly drowned out by the sound of the engine.

Honig, on the other hand, maintained his usual silly smile and waved as they drove along. He'd partake in the banter tomorrow.

Chapter 3 - Maintenance

29 August 2431 – 07:56

Honig stepped into the station as usual, already in his navy-blue uniform and four minutes early. As always, he said hello to the secretary who worked front desk as she unlocked the door for him. Despite having known her for nearly two years, he couldn't remember her name. Stepping around the corner, he leaned against the wall, arms crossed.

"How's the lovely lady doing today?"

She smiled. "Fairly good. Yourself?"

"Positively dapper. What's on the to-do list for today?"

"Chief wants to see you."

"Uh oh," Honig widened his eyes exaggeratedly. "What does he want?"

"Didn't say. He didn't seem to be in a great mood this morning."

"Oh." The silly smile faded a bit from Honig's face. "Huh."

"I don't think you have anything to worry about." The secretary smiled at him reassuringly.

"Aight, off I go then!"

Stepping into the main hallway, the first person he saw was Shepard with a clipboard, already in his full police armor.

"Two minutes late, as always?"

"No, good sir. Four minutes early!" answered Honig. It had become a running joke throughout parts of the department about Honig always being exactly two minutes late. His exchange with the secretary each morning assured this.

When Honig reached the chief's office, he knocked briefly before letting himself in and sitting down. Chief Eckhart looked at Honig for a moment. Anyone lesser he'd reprimand for not waiting to be offered a seat. Theoretically, he should do the same for Honig, but there were more pressing matters to attend to.

"Morning!" said Honig in his usual cheerful demeanor. In this case, he was hoping to defuse the rumored bad mood the chief was in.

"Morning." Eckhart looked at Honig for a moment. "UV-4, when was the last time you had to work on it?"

Honig had to think. "Utility Vehicle 4" was the official name for his tank, though no one referred to it that way. Finally, he answered. "Oil change a few weeks back. One of the spokes was looking shady, so I was preparing to replace that."

"I already have Hershall working on that." He turned back and forth in his chair uneasily. "How is its load?"

Honig looked at Eckhart, confused.

"The main gun and the coaxial, how are those doing?"

Honig raised bushy white eyebrows. "Six rounds of HE for the 100mm, the coaxial has no ammunition on board." Honig's expression turned serious. "Is there something I should be aware of, sir?"

"No," Eckhart answered quickly. "Keeping track of inventory. Inspections." He rubbed his eyes. He looked tired. "I want you to take UV-4 out today. Take this to the armory and get what you need to outfit it fully first." He slid a requisition order across his desk with his signature on it. "Bring it up north to the power plant. Should be a nice drive," continued Eckhart, his voice attempting to sound cheerful but his expression dead.

"Alright... Have a good day, sir." Honig stood up slowly, picking up the requisition order. He then saluted and stepped out of the office, looking at the order. He considered what had just happened for a few moments until the nervous feeling in the pit of his stomach gave way to routines and procedures he'd learned long ago. He'd need a few guys to help carry the shells. If the armory had a munitions cart, that would be better. With a cart, they could also carry out the ammo cans for the coaxial in one trip. Without it, it'd just take longer.

Looking down the hallway, he called over Shepard. "We got work to do. Also, grab Thomas."

"Shit, this early?"

"Yeah, meet me at the armory. We have a few things to pick up."

"Got it." Shepard gave Honig a thumbs up and turned to find Tom.

A few minutes later, Honig had reached the armory. The building itself had two, one for the Earth Union Civil Enforcement office and one for the Novus Public Protection office. The building served as the primary station for both departments, something which was unique to this world. Both armories were nearly the same, located in reinforced parts of the building with concrete floors and blast-proof doors. When Honig stepped in, the quartermaster greeted him. He was an old sergeant, growing fat with age and ill-shaven. Today, he wore an olive drab t-shirt and navy trousers. Not a well-kept appearance, but then again, he wasn't someone typically interacting with the general public.

"How can I help you today?" He sat up straighter in his chair, pushing aside his computer console.

"An unusual order…" Honig slid the requisition slip under the see-through metal mesh that stood between him and the armory. The quartermaster took it and looked at it for a moment.

"You serious, man?"

"Yeah."

"Nothing personal, but give me a minute. I want to double-check with the chief on this one." He picked up his phone and called. A few seconds later, he put it back down. "Well, we only have eleven more 100mm rounds for you, and I can only spare two cans of 8mm." He paused. "Is everything alright?"

"Eckhart seemed on edge about something. Not my call."

"Right then, let me take you in back. We'll use the big door to get everything out. You need help?"

"I've got two more guys coming. I think we'll be good."

Soon Shepard and Tom arrived. While they began loading the munitions cart, Honig proceeded out to the vehicle yard behind the station, then into the garage where the tank was kept. As Chief Eckhart said, Hershall was already working on it, trying to pull a wheel off while two other officers watched in amusement.

As Honig stopped next to them, Hershall turned around, perspiration on his brow. "How, the fuck, do you get these things off?"

"You're young." Honig gestured back towards to wheel. At this, Hershall just rolled his eyes and went back to pulling on it. Stepping around, Honig found the issue. "The center pin there, on the axle, twist that."

Hershall did as he was told, and the wheel slid off.

"You have much to learn of the way of metal and wheels, young one."

Hershall sighed audibly. He was one of the few "young" guys in the department who knew anything about this vehicle, which was a point of pride for him. He didn't necessarily enjoy humor pertaining to his knowledge on the subject.

"But for now, I need you for heavy lifting."

Hershall looked over towards the station, and spotting the fully loaded munitions cart approaching, exclaimed, "What in the world!?"

They spent the next hour loading ammunition into the tank's turret, with Hershall on top handing shells down to Honig, who then loaded them into the ready rack. As they did this, a group of Novian officers gathered at the edge of the motor yard, gawking and joking at the activities at hand. Two others, who appeared to be the most senior, just stood in serious silence.

By 09:00, they had finished their task and were prepping to leave, the tank's engine left to idle. Honig now had his standard-issue sidearm in a holster on his side, which was unusual for him. However, he still refrained from donning an armored suit, which left his pistol belt uncomfortably loose. He pulled himself up using the handholds on the side of the turret, then dropping himself into the commander's hatch. Shepard was already halfway out of the second hatch, located just to the right of Honig's. They would make sure that they did not bump into anything on the way out, as the driver's view, even with the front hatch open, wasn't great.

"Yo, Honig!" One of the Novian officers shouted as they started to pull forward. "What're your plans for today?"

"Hunting," answered Honig, his usual loony smile across his face. His docile expression hid an uneasy feeling that something wasn't right with the day.

Chapter 4 – Confrontation

"How do I activate thermal again?" asked Shepard. He was sitting in the gunner position adjusting the targeting computer.

"It should be that white switch on the right," answered Honig, turning away from the main gun's breach.

"Already tried that."

Honig stopped what he was doing and leaned forward over Shepard's shoulder, looking over the controls. "Yeah, it should be…" He adjusted the switch himself, changing from standard to infrared, and then the screen turned black. "Oh." He switched back to infrared, then forward again. "Thermal's out." He made another note on his PDA. "Well then, just go through the rest of the settings. See if you can't find anything else wrong."

"Sure thing."

They had arrived at the power plant roughly thirty minutes before, and rather than continuing along their usual route north of the plant towards the hills, they had stopped here for a bit. Honig had decided that it'd be good to do a full check of the tank's systems. It was likely that this thing had never been fully tested since its arrival on Echelon, as police operations did not typically bring said systems into use.

Honig turned on the three loader's displays, each of which provided diagnostic information on the tank's weapons systems as well as ammunition status and requests from the gunner. In this case, most results were showing as empty or malfunctioning. This was expected. Before its service in the CE, it had been stripped down to a bare minimum of equipment, and for the first time, this fact was made painfully obvious. He then looked down despairingly at the bolt holes in the turret's floor that would normally secure an autoloader. He was the only one here who knew how to load the gun manually, and those shells were heavy. Looking back up at breach, he pulled the loading lever down with a smooth, albeit heavy, click. The breach slid open, and the ejector kicked out, looking to remove a shell that wasn't there.

"Good, good."

Leaning forward and to the right past the breach, he inspected the co-axial, a boxy Benning's Firearms Group heavy machine gun modified to work with the automatic systems housed in the front of the turret. However, like so much else, the reloading mechanism had been removed. So, Honig began the process of pulling an ammo can into place.

He was then interrupted by the voice of Hershall over the internal comms. "Sir, someone's here to see you."

"What?"

Honig leaned back, trying to relax his stiff muscles, then slowly proceeded to a standing position, bringing himself up and out of the commander's hatch. Turning left, he was surprised to see an Earth Union soldier in full battle gear, standing at attention. Unlike the CE office, his armor was dark green and reinforced, classified as "Infantry Standard." Honig recognized the markings on his gear as Echelon Reserve Recon, a corporal.

"How are you doing today, sir?" asked the corporal, more of a formality than anything else.

"Fine, what-" Honig was then cut off.

"What are you doing here?"

Honig furrowed his brow. He didn't appreciate such a young reservist questioning him. "Making sure our tank still works. What are you doing here?"

"Can't say, sir." The corporal looked over the tank. "How long are you going to be here?"

"Is there something going on here that I should know about, Corporal?" Honig straightened his posture, looking down at him.

The corporal stared back through his black lenses. "I'm going to have to ask you to leave this area, sir."

Honig watched as the soldier tightened his grip on his rifle. They were technically on the same side, but the soldier staring back at him had something else on his mind.

Honig would find out later. For now, it'd be best to end the confrontation. He turned to face forward towards the driver's hatch, located below the front of the turret.

"Hershall, let's get back to the station."

Hershall nodded and dropped down into the driver's position, closing the hatch. Shepard had since come up and out of the secondary hatch to see what was going on. As they pulled forward, they watched as the corporal turned to run towards the brush line. It was unlikely that he was alone. At a minimum, the rest of his squad had to be lurking around here somewhere.

"What was that about?" asked Shepard, his expression concerned.

"I don't know. We'll go back to the station and get this sorted out." Honig then ducked back down into the turret, activating the internal comms. "Hershall, take the fast route."

"Lights and sirens, sir?"

Honig considered it but quickly decided against it. Better not to attract more attention to themselves than a tank speeding down the main road already did. "No, just move quickly."

Chapter 5 - Turn

29 August 2431 – 11:00 – Police Station

Chief Eckhart sat at his desk, concentrating on the papers in front of him. The meeting that took place the previous morning did not yield good news. As it turned out, the armed forces planned on the Civil Enforcement office playing a major role in the urban areas. Eckhart wasn't sure if his men would be able to do that.

The papers that spread across his desk were full reports on the department's readiness as a whole: personnel count, ammunition, body armor, state of emergency planning, fall back areas. Overall, the local CE office had 49 active-duty officers, with an additional 39 personnel that could be called in. Officers from other cities would not be available to assist. They had their own problems to deal with. As for ammunition and armor, not enough.

Pushing his own department's logistics reports aside, he re-examined a report on the Novus Public Protection office's strength. 45 active-duty officers, with over 50 that could be called in. Furthermore, they were more than well-equipped when it came to ammunition. As for armor, he lacked that information. Technically the report was out of date by nearly two months, but not much could have changed since then. Hopefully.

He brought his hands up to the sides of his face, massaging his temples. The plan was simple enough. At midnight, the CE office would take over dispatch, quietly. They would then immediately put out a ready call to all available active duty and reserve officers. If everything worked out, they would have full control by 0300, and none would be the wiser. Furthermore, no one would get hurt. He repeated this phrase in his head, trying to cool himself down.

"No one would get hurt."

His thoughts were then interrupted by heavy footsteps coming down the hall. Looking up, he saw one of Novus' officers in full combat armor with a rifle slung across his chest, walking past slowly.

"Fuck!" Eckhart ducked behind his desk, reaching for his handgun and pulling out his cellphone. The footsteps seemed to fade down the hall. But did they? He couldn't be sure, and his racing heart wasn't making things any easier. Staying hidden, Eckhart dialed the number of his best lieutenant. After a few agonizing seconds, he finally picked up.

"They've found out. Move forward with the plan now!"

Chapter 6 - Standoff

29 August 2431 – 11:43

"UV-4 to dispatch," repeated Honig. Nothing but static was coming back. "Shepard, if you could pull on that antenna for me. See if it's loose." Halfway back from the plant, Honig had elected to contact dispatch about their encounter with the corporal. To his knowledge, there were no drills that day. Typically, both departments were notified when such things were going to occur – especially when it pertained to the city's only source of power. The radio, or perhaps the network as a whole, didn't seem to be operational. Come to think of it, he hadn't heard any traffic since they had left the station less than three hours before. It wouldn't have been the first time the radio network went down, but it had been a while since it last happened. Since the new towers went up, communications had been nearly flawless.

"It's on there tight," reported Shepard, pulling himself back into the secondary hatch. "You want me to give 'em a call?"

"Yeah, tell them the radio's down, and we're on our way back. I'll talk to them about the plant once we're there."

Shepard already had his phone out and was dialing the non-emergency line. The phone system was a constant in the universe. It didn't go down. While Shepard did this,

26

Honig looked over the city. They were entering the industrial district's outskirts, high ground from which the whole city could be seen. First, there were the roofs of warehouses, the closest structures to the plant. A little farther down were the factories and offices, the only truly solid structures in the city, constructed of reinforced concrete rather than the thin steel of the housing district. The housing district was on the horizon. The oldest houses had shiny domed roofs, leftovers from when people did not know if the atmosphere here was safe to venture into and everything was airtight. The newer homes could be distinguished by their flatter black roofing, far closer to what one would expect on Earth. The city had considered outfitting the structures here with solar panels on the roofs, but the near-constant cloud cover would have rendered them useless. The far edge of the city was hidden by a thick white haze, typical of this planet. Not that there was much to see over there. The southernmost parts of the housing district stopped at the marshes. His view was then blocked the rest of the way by large buildings as they descended among the warehouses.

"Anything?" asked Honig, turning to Shepard.

"Just ringing. Nobody's picking up."

"You try the secretary?"

"Yeah, 'phone not available' for her." Shepard looked at Honig, a mix of annoyance and concern across his face. "I mean, dispatch isn't always on the ball, but come on! Someone over there should be answering!"

27

Honig sighed, though it couldn't be heard over the roar of the tank's engine. "We'll be there soon enough, and it's about lunchtime."

"This is weird," continued Shepard.

Honig nodded, then leaned forward, staring down the road. This was probably a mix up with communications, some error on dispatch's end causing the system to go down. If Chief Eckhart hadn't been so on edge this morning, Honig would be more likely to believe that.

Soon enough, they had entered the industrial district, electing to cut directly through the loading areas rather than go around. As they drove through, there were fewer workers present than usual, and those that were seemed hesitant to acknowledge the massive armored vehicle driving through their midst. In a larger, more established city, this could be seen as normal. Around here, though, the two police departments had established good relations with the civilian populace.

It took another twenty minutes to navigate the rest of the way through the industrial district. Another five minutes of driving finally brought them past City Center and onto Main Street. Just two more turns, and they'd be at the station on 2nd. Unlike the suspicious glances from the workers in the industrial district, the few people here seemed to scatter at the sight of them.

"What in the world is going on?" Honig said aloud, watching as people ran inside nearby buildings. He got his answer when they turned the corner.

Among the eight police cars barricading the road to the station at both ends, the entirety of the Novus Public Protection Office seemed to be out front. Nearly all of them were in full armor, carrying the bullpup rifles normally reserved for the Novian military. Most were set up behind makeshift cover aiming at the police station, with the remainder stationed by the barricades blocking entry to the street.

Upon seeing the tank come around the corner, a number of them shouted, some pointing their rifles while others ducked for cover. Honig and Shepard froze, trying to comprehend the scene unfolding in front of them. Coming to his senses, Honig finally ducked, pulling Shepard down with him and slamming their respective hatches shut.

"Get in the gunner's position!"

"What's even going on!?"

"I don't know!" Honig proceeded to turn on all the tank's systems in a single rapid motion. By the time he activated the commander override, Shepard was still fumbling with the controls. Pushing himself forward over Shepard's shoulder, he started the remaining gunner controls with another sweep of his hand. "Whatever you do, DO NOT fire, you hear me!?"

"Yeah, yeah."

Honig then backed up and, realizing he'd forgotten something, cursed loudly. Turning on the internal comms, he shouted, "Hershall, You alright? Close your hatch!"

Thankfully, the voice of Hershall came back over the intercom. "I'm here, hatch's closed."

"Get ready to move, ok?"

"Roger!"

Honig stood up in the commander's cupola, looking out through the viewports. Fortunately, it appeared that the Novian officers were just as shocked to see them and were only just beginning to regroup. Most were aiming at the tank now, though it would be a futile effort – none of their weapons could even hope to damage this thing if they chose to fire. Looking down into the front of the turret, Honig's heart jumped. He'd never finished loading the coaxial. Ducking down again, he grabbed the radio with one hand while he fumbled to get a grip on the ammunition belt with the other.

"CE Captain Honig to dispatch, can anyone hear me?" Without an immediate response, he threw down the mic and focused on loading the coaxial. "Breath, you've done this a hundred times before." He pulled back the charging lever on the machine gun while feeding the ammunition belt into its left side. Once he felt it click in, he released it, concluding the process.

"Coaxial ready!" He slid back to his position in the cupola, grabbing the radio mic and peering out the viewports. "CE Captain Honig here. Can I get an update on the situation?"

This time, an unfamiliar voice responded, "Novian Command to Captain Honig, exit your vehicle immediately."

Honig didn't even bother responding. Putting the mic down, he observed a group of Novian officers coordinating at the edge of the street before entering a building.

"Hershall, back this thing up to the next intersection, don't let them get close." Honig's training had finally kicked in, and his tone of panic was giving way to one of cold calculation. Despite popular belief, armored vehicles were remarkably vulnerable when unsupported. Even a few ill-equipped individuals could do nasty things to this tank if they could get on top of it.

Seconds later, they had positioned themselves in the middle of the three-way intersection, a building to their back, the blockade in front of them, and open streets on either side.

"Shepard, left side!"

They turned the turret to face the new arrival, a rapidly approaching Novian police vehicle. The vehicle driver must have panicked upon realizing that he was the focus of the tank's massive gun. It turned left, hard, and with a crash, flipped onto its side, sliding a short way across the pavement.

"Do not fire." Honig repeated. His nerves were fine, but he was worried about Shepard, who currently exercised full control over the tank's weaponry.

Turning away from the crash, Honig looked back towards the blockade. They were probably communicating with the crew of the crashed vehicle via radio. This was a problem as suddenly Honig and his crew were near surrounded. He then spotted a few officers in the corner building to the tank's left, trying to get close enough to make a rush at them.

"Shepard, quarter turn right, building corner!"

They caught four of the officers in the open, staring up the barrel of the tank's 100mm. Two dropped their rifles, raising their hands and backing up slowly. Another froze. The fourth made a run for it back to the barricade.

"Shepard, hold your fire…" Honig looked around at the developing situation. Novus had gotten too close too quickly. Without firing upon them, it'd be hard to convince them to stay back, and he didn't have enough information to justify that. "Hershall, back this thing up to Main Street."

The hull of the tank rotated left, tearing up pavement beneath it. All the while, the turret maintained its aim on the three officers still in the street. Soon enough, they'd backed up to Main Street, stopping in the middle of the road perpendicular to the flow of traffic. Looking up the street, Honig cringed as an electric bus slammed on its brakes and turned to avoid slamming into them.

Looking right, Honig spotted another Novian police vehicle a little over a hundred meters down the street. It had pulled over, and its officers were disembarking, all armed. The left side was still clear, aside from a few of the bus's angry passengers getting out to yell at them. Again, it'd be best to find a place where it'd be difficult for Novus to get close. While Main Street was substantially wider than 2nd, it still wasn't wide enough to make Honig comfortable.

"Hershall, bring us back to City Center."

"Got it!"

They turned left and activated their sirens, quickly persuading those in front of them to get out of the way.

City Center featured the town green, a turf field approximately 300 by 300 meters in size with a fountain in the middle. That'd be big enough to give Honig the reaction time he'd need to keep anyone away from the tank's hull. Within minutes they'd reached it, and they drove through the decorative chain fence around its edge, proceeding to park next to the fountain in the middle. Looking around again, all appeared to be clear, for now. Honig activated the internal comms, talking to both Shepard and Hershall.

"Either of you have family on-world?"

Shepard turned and shook his head. Hershall answered no.

"I know neither of you are married, but if you have any girlfriends or people that matter to you, try and contact them now. Tell them to stay indoors until further notice."

After peering out the viewports one more time, Honig turned to his radio, setting it to emergency and military frequencies.

"This is Civil Enforcement Captain Honig to any Earth Union personnel. We are under attack! I repeat, we are under attack by Novian forces!"

Chapter 7 – Rain

30 August 2431 – 08:00

Honig ran his hand across his brow, attempting to stave off an impending headache. Apparently, a war had started. The previous night the Civil Enforcement Office had managed to negotiate a ceasefire with the Novus Public Protection office. Or maybe it was the other way around. It depended on who you asked. Regardless, through god's will alone, no one was killed in those first tense hours the day before. Now it was a matter of maintaining that excellent record.

CE equipment lined both sides of the street, and officers could be seen patrolling roofs of surrounding buildings. Most everyone else was inside their vehicles. Aside from the sound of falling rain, everything was silent. It reminded Honig of a funeral procession. He looked up at the dark grey sky, directing some of the rainwater off the back of his helmet. He and his crew had gotten no sleep the previous night, not that anyone did. After retreating from the police station, the first hour was spent in the City Center, staring down anyone who dared to even look at their vehicle. Eventually, Honig and his crew elected to leave the city limits and try to find a suitable position at the edge of the plains. It was on their way out that they finally met up with another unit of CE personnel and learned of the situation at hand.

The common consensus, formulated through a mix of rumor and speculation, was that Novus had declared war on the Earth Union at some point within the last week. Word of this development had supposedly reached the upper levels of the armed forces on-world, but for one reason or another, neither side had decided to act, not until yesterday at least. Where the Earth Union Echelon reserve battalions were was still unknown. The same could be said for the armored company that Novus supposedly had ready to take this city by storm. For now, Police Chief Eckhart would be meeting with the director of the local Novus Public Protection Office to make a plan going forward for this city. All that was left to do now was wait.

Honig looked back down along the street, pulling on his shoulder straps in an attempt to relieve the weight of his armor. It had been quite a while since Honig had donned full protection, and this wasn't even his set. His armor was stuck in a locker somewhere in the police station, and it was unlikely that he'd be recovering it given the current circumstances. The armor he was wearing was designed for a more muscular individual. The back upper-torso plate was edging on too wide so that the shoulder armor hung limply from its attachment points on the breastplate. At least the helmet fit, the head's up display inside the goggles lining up correctly when he chose to use it.

"Would you like a raincoat, sir?" asked Shepard, approaching him. He was already wearing one over his armor and had a second one hanging from his arm.

36

"Yes, please." Honig took the raincoat, shaking off some accumulated raindrops before unfolding it. It was more like a thin black plastic bedsheet. He then began to pull the ungainly thing over his head, only for it to get stuck at every opportunity.

"Let me help you with that." Shepard stepped forward, pulling on the raincoat just enough to get it the rest of the way over Honig's helmet.

Honig looked down at his feet. He had been through too much to need someone helping him get a raincoat on. He kept his mouth shut, though. He then looked up at the tank, watching rainwater drip down its massive black and white hull and onto the street.

"Now we wait," Honig muttered, watching as another officer approached. He had a pile of rifles in his arms.

"Better take one. We don't know how this is going to end," stated the officer.

Honig nodded and picked one from the top of the pile. It was a STORM 1 rifle, standard issue in the previous war between Earth and Novus. He was thoroughly familiar with the model. He rotated it side to side, looking it over. Props to the quartermaster: While certainly well used, there was not a speck of rust on it. The officer then handed Honig a sling, which he promptly connected to the rifle, followed by an extra magazine.

"Excellent." He stared at the officer until he got the hint and moved along.

"A penny for your thoughts?" asked Shepard.

"Nothing to think about." Honig sighed. He slung the rifle across his chest before bringing it around to his right side.

It was another hour before Chief Eckhart returned. Upon arrival, he immediately called over the entirety of the CE office's command staff. They all followed the Chief into their "command center," a coffee shop that the department frequented before this mess.

Eckhart stepped behind the register counter at the back of the shop, his hands on its surface and leaning forward heavily. All the color seemed to have left his face, and his eyes were dark with fatigue. The body armor he wore pulled his shoulders down, emphasizing his sorry state.

"Sit."

Everyone sat down, pulling chairs from next to tables. Some tried to make order of the mess. Others just sat down as quickly as they could. Honig didn't bother with the chairs, instead sitting down in a booth on the shop's far side.

"Gentlemen…" Eckhart inhaled heavily through his nose. "It is true. War has officially been declared against Novus. I have negotiated a ceasefire with the Novus Public

Protection Office, which will last, starting now, through tomorrow. Please bear in mind, however, this agreement is only between us and the Public Protection Office. For all intents and purposes, this does not apply to NAF or our own military."

At this, there was a visible shift in the mood of the room. Honig frowned. This couldn't work without Novus Armed Forces onboard. One of the officers stood up to speak but was quickly silenced by a piercing glance from Eckhart.

Eckhart continued, "So, it will stand from this point on you are not to approach Novian personnel unless absolutely necessary. They reserve the right to protect themselves just as we do, and remember; we are no longer friends with them." He stopped for a moment breathing in deeply, pressing his eyes shut, trying to remember something. "As such," he exhaled. "We have divided the city into areas of control, which will be maintained until tomorrow at midnight. We will not encroach upon their territory, and they have agreed not to encroach upon ours. We are passing word along to representatives of our armed forces regarding this plan. Novus should be doing the same."

A sergeant near the front then stood up, visibly frustrated. "Sir, it is our duty as members of the Earth Union to take and hold this city. If Novus wishes to pull out, they may, but we shouldn't allow them to hold ground here. This is our city."

A visible twitch distorted Eckhart's face momentarily, but he otherwise maintained his composure. "Sit down, Sergeant." They stared at each other for a moment before the sergeant finally backed off. Eckhart then continued, "We are evacuating the city. Given current circumstances and what we expect to happen, this will be the best option. However, we lack the resources to take care of the people…"

The whole room tensed up.

"So, we will be putting the entire civilian population, both ours and theirs, under Novus' care."

At this, parts of the room erupted. "What the fuck are we here for!?" One of the older sergeants stood up. Honig recognized him as one of the department's veterans. He had fought in the previous war against Novus. "First we let those bastards sit here in our city, and now we're giving up our own people? What the fuck do we even stand for?"

Another officer stood up, fists clenched. "Why in God's name would you do this? We have one fucking job, and the second things go bad, we just give up? Who the fuck are you?"

Eckhart didn't back down, instead standing straighter, though he lacked the height advantage. "Though we still maintain a military advantage over Novus' Police forces, when the real fighting starts, we lack the ability to house this city's population."

"Why are we even evacuating?" countered the veteran.

"Our own armed forces would prefer it that way."

This silenced the room. From a military perspective, essentially getting rid of the civilian population would be beneficial. One less draw on resources, and it would be easier taking and holding ground when in-city civilian shelters were not a consideration. Another unspoken aspect of the situation was that Novus was truly better equipped for mass civilian care, having substantially more in the way of emergency shelters than the Earth Union. Not that the civilian population would be that much better off under Novus's care. All the emergency shelters on-world wouldn't be enough when winter came.

"Lastly, we are not to inform the civilian population that they will be under Novus's supervision. I'm sure you all understand why."

The meeting did not continue for much longer after that, mostly covering the specifics of the zones of control. Fortunately, for Eckhart's sake, most of the officers in the room did not wish to fight Novus. Though it was left unsaid, multiple officers here had friends and family that were, in fact, Novian. The same could be said for Novus' officers. The population of this world had intermingled enough that prior to this point, the difference between Earth and Novian citizenship didn't seem like much more than different tax codes.

After the meeting's conclusion, Honig got up and approached Eckhart. He was still behind the register counter, now looking over a map of the lower city with his lieutenants.

"Sir."

Eckhart looked up. "Yes, Honig?"

"How long have we known about this, and how come I was never briefed?" Honig eyed the lieutenants to his left and right. It was clear that they'd known something.

Eckhart looked at the lieutenants, then dismissed them with a wave of his hand. Once they'd stepped out of the building, Eckhart looked Honig directly in the eyes. "You and I both know that your rank here was intended as a reward for your prior service. Your assignment here was meant to be an easy one. We never meant to drag you into this."

Though Honig knew this to be true, it did not prevent the swell of anger building up inside of him. He wasn't expecting Eckhart to be so blunt and lacked a response.

Finally, Eckhart continued, "We still don't know how this is going to end. There is still time to step down. You've done your duty. You don't owe us anything."

"I think I'll continue to serve," answered Honig through his teeth.

Eckhart stared at him for another moment, his expression changing from one ready for confrontation to almost sad. "Good luck out there."

Honig nodded and then stepped out.

Chapter 8 – The Walk

30 August 2431 – 11:00

Honig, his crew, and three other CE units were assigned to the evacuation of the central housing block. As its name indicated, it represented the current center of the southern half of the city, located just south of the police station and City Center. The rain had since ceased, and while it wouldn't make operations any easier, it was a nice change of pace. Thus far, at least in the Earth Union's areas of operation, panic had been kept to a minimum. Truly the best thing to do in this situation was to keep everyone moving quickly, and Earth Union CE forces excelled at this.

The other three CE units were composed of two officers and a squad car each. Less personnel for starting evacuation of a street than was preferable, but the situation at hand was stretching the department thin. Honig and his crew were assigned their usual position, manning the department's main battle tank. They remained at the ends of the streets, waiting to be called on if the need arose. Shepard was providing the extra manpower, repeatedly jumping down from the tank's turret to assist the other units with whatever was needed. Honig and Hershall always remained behind. If Advanced Enforcement was needed, the tank had been equipped with a large plow on the front. To put it discreetly, the plow wasn't necessarily intended to deal with debris. Fortunately, it looked like this would not be needed, not that there were enough people here to make effective use of it anyway.

This process continued for the next five hours. Start at the end of a street and order families out of their homes one at a time. Rinse and repeat until the assigned area had been cleared. As other neighborhoods were evacuated and there were fewer areas to cover, CE presence became more concentrated. This was beneficial for just about everyone involved, as the last few streets were substantially rowdier than the first, having been alerted of the impending situation by word of mouth and the obvious presence of CE personnel en masse.

Honig and his crew concluded their operations at the southern end of the central housing block, moving up to the eastern edge within sight of Novus' roadblocks. While CE forces had been performing evacuations, Novus had set up a border, using it to briefly screen civilians before ushering them further east towards the hills where the emergency camps were to be set up. Now that evacuations were concluded, the border served as a defensive line. Honig looked it over. It was composed primarily of Public Protection vehicles parked across the road and light barricades with numerous NPP officers spread out between them.

Ducking down into his hatch, Honig ordered, "Hold here for a minute."

Popping back out, he started his slow climb down the left side of the turret, dropping down off the side of the hull the rest of the way to the pavement. Shepard came up halfway out of his hatch, keeping an eye on him. Hershall, on the other hand, kept his hatch shut, watching through the tank's front viewports. Honig straightened his posture and walked towards the Novian line, removing his helmet and carrying it at his side. As he approached, more eyes turned on him, the old man of the Earth Union. When he came within ten meters of the barricades, one of the Novian officers stepped forward to meet him. Honig recognized the officer. They knew each other as acquaintances through the occasional passing in the street or in the halls of the police station.

"How you doing?"

"Been better," answered the officer.

"You all set here?"

"Yeah, we're good."

They stood silently for a moment, listening to the sound of idling engines.

"You stay safe alright?" said Honig.

"Yeah." They shook hands. "Hopefully, we meet again under better circumstances, eh?"

"Hopefully."

Chapter 9 – Storm Front

30 August 2431 – 01:13

Honig awoke to the sound of voices outside the tent. He wiped a layer of sweat from his brow. Though it was cool outside, it was also incredibly humid – a fact emphasized by the stifling nature of this tent. Part of the agreement with the Novus Public Protection office was that both parties would back off from the city rather than risk confrontation at midnight when the peace agreement ended. Thus, the CE office had set up camp in the grassy fields west of the city. As far as they knew, Novus had set up on the opposite side of the valley, though they were likely far busier given that they were taking care of the freshly evacuated civilian population.

Reaching over to his right, he picked up his phone, tapping on the screen and turning it on. 01:15. He rubbed his eyes, pissed to have been woken up. Listening for another minute, he came to the conclusion that the hushed tones of the voices outside were urgent enough to warrant investigation. As quickly as he could, he pulled his heavy combat boots on, then getting up and opening the tent flap. At least half of the personnel here were outside their tents, all looking up at the sky. Finally, Honig looked up. The cloud cover overhead had thinned a bit, and throughout the black sky there were flashes emanating through the haze.

"What in the blazes?"

"Satellites."

Honig looked over. Officer Weiss was standing near him.

"They're taking out the satellites. Each of the flashes is a missile hitting," Weiss continued.

Honig looked back up just in time to see a particularly bright flash, followed by a low rumble.

"Fuck." Weiss started rubbing his chin. "That had to be a ship getting hit, possibly its reactor going critical. Nothing else would make a sound like that."

They watched the sky for another few minutes, but nothing more came of the larger flash. Keeping track of orbital and aeronautical events was a hobby of Weiss'. On any given day, he could give a fairly accurate assessment of the number of craft overhead, ranging from in atmosphere to high-orbit. He even went as far as investing in an orbital monitor, an expensive piece of equipment that utilized a series of antenna set up around its operational area to find and track extraordinarily far away objects. Unfortunately for Weiss, he had to leave most of his equipment behind during the evacuation of the city, and that represented a significant investment sitting unguarded in his home. A few personnel in the CE office were making bets on how long it would take for Weiss to sneak back into the city to try and retrieve at least some of his gear.

Honig watched another flash before feeling the pull of fatigue set back in. "I'm going back to sleep."

Weiss nodded, not taking his eyes of the sky.

Chapter 10 – LZ South

31 August 2431 – 10:00

The morning had been busy thus far. Elements of the Echelon Reserve 1st Motorized Company had arrived, composed of a platoon of troops, three armored personnel carriers and a scout car. The rumor now was that there were substantially more in the way of Earth Union armed forces on the sides of the hills opposite the city, but they did not wish to reveal their hand to Novus quite yet. Not that there was much to see. A thicker than usual fog bank had moved in obscuring most of the valley, and it was starting to rain again.

Upon arrival, the motorized company ordered that the CE Office pack up their camp immediately. Though they were trying to hide it, it was obvious that they were setting up these fields as landing zones. The edges of each field had been lined with portable beacons for landing computers to lock on to, and a team of engineers was searching the ground for soft spots. Meanwhile, CE personnel had been set to work assisting in the digging of trench lines through the mud on the slopes facing the city, roughly half a kilometer in front of said landing fields. No one was happy about it, but they knew what was coming.

The relationship between the Civil Enforcement office and the Earth Union armed forces was an interesting one. The CE office was technically a branch of the armed forces, though in most cases it operated independently from the other branches. After the first civil war, the CE was put in place to, alongside policing the populace, be capable of putting down potential revolution, and in time of war, serve as a tactical asset within urban areas. How realistic it was for the CE office serving as a tactical asset was open to debate. As seen here on Echelon, they had elected to fall back rather than engage in open warfare with the opposing side. For obvious reasons, this had rather incredibly pissed off the Earth Union Armed Forces in the immediate area. Rather than having the city already under control, they instead had a large urban area in limbo and not enough forces to reliably take and hold it until reinforcements arrived. There would be hell to pay, but that would come later. For now, the current situation was far more pressing.

Honig had been exempted from the digging, both because of his age and his rank. Instead, he and Hershall had been set to "prepare the tank for hostilities." Shepard wouldn't be joining them, however. He'd been grabbed to assist in the digging. As for the tank, the only further preparations that could really be done to it would be loading it the rest of the way with ammunition, of which there was none. Aside from a single can of 8mm, the Motorized Company was unable to provide anything more in the way of supplies, especially 100mm shells which were needed most.

Upon request from the motorized company's commanding officer, Hershall and Honig moved their tank forward to the trench lines, overlooking the fields between them and the city. Theoretically, in the event of a first strike from Novus, they'd be providing fire support until the remainder of 1st Motorized arrived. Of course, the overall appearance of it was rather ludicrous, the massive black and white hull sticking out like a sore thumb on the dark green hill. An assignment of this type was new for Hershall, not so much for Honig.

Honig stood in the Commander's hatch, his posture perfect as he procedurally scanned the valley below. Hershall, on the other hand, sat cross legged on top of the turret to Honig's right. His arms were crossed, his raincoat covering the entirety of him and rendering him a black shapeless blob. Honig's raincoat remained inside the turret. Being around other Earth Union armed forces was reviving his old ways. The rain jacket was bulky and would impair his ability to operate should he have to duck back in and take control suddenly. Regardless of how wet he'd get, he'd earned the ire of the men below him, shoveling their way through the mud.

After half an hour, Hershall stirred. "I'm not sure that the evacuation of the city was such a good idea," he remarked sullenly, turning his head slightly to the left. "The city is the only shelter within a hundred kilometers of here, and winter is not that far off."

Honig leaned back against the edge of the hatch, turning to Hershall. "What are we to do about it?"

Hershall shrugged, demoralized.

Honig looked back down into the valley at the white wall of fog. "My house is still there."

"Fuck..." Hershall drew out the word slowly, bringing his hands to the sides of his head.

"Yeah. I never managed to get anything out of my house either."

Hershall was now rocking back and forth ever so slightly. Clearly a topic that he did not need to be reminded of. He then slapped his right hand down on the top of the turret. "There has to be some way to get down there. 'Riot patrol,' maybe? I don't want some fucking looter going through my shit."

Honig raised his eyebrows, the idea was tempting. "Perhaps if..." He stopped there. Going down into the city would definitely result in himself and or Hershall getting shot, either by Novus, or by Earth Union Armed Forces for "desertion."

"Hmm?" Hershall turned around hopefully.

"Sorry, no," said Honig, frowning.

Hershall didn't bother responding, instead returning to his forward-facing position.

"You know it'd be a bad idea. Best to play it safe for now."

"Yeah."

Honig paused a moment, watching the men below him dig. "The secretary, what's her name?"

"Helen I think it was? Why?"

"I wonder where she is right now."

"I never got to know her, unfortunately."

Honig raised an eyebrow. "Really?"

"Buzzed me in every morning, that's it."

"Huh."

Honig stood up straighter again, looking back down into the valley. Down the hill, he spotted some faint movement through the fog.

"Hershall, our eleven." Honig pointed with his right hand while reaching for the radio with his left. As Hershall scrambled down to the front hatch, Honig keyed the mic. "UV-1 to command, movement spotted east of our position, 100 meters out."

"Command, received. Can you identify what it is?"

"Negative. We're working on that now."

The tank shook as Hershall attempted to start the engine. Technically it should have been running this entire time, but Honig had let it slip. A lapse in judgement. Hopefully they wouldn't end up paying for it. The men in the trench had heard Honig over the radio and had since thrown down their shovels, picking up their rifles and taking up positions along the line. One of the corporals then proceeded to climb up the left side of the tank's turret, coming up next to Honig.

"Point 'em out for me."

"Our eleven, down there," said Honig, pointing.

The corporal then opened a panel on his left gauntlet, adjusting his helmet's optics to zoom in on the position. He then brought his right hand up to the side of his helmet, activating his squad comms.

"Target marked," said the Corporal, before jumping back down off the turret.

Honig reached down into the turret, pulling out his own combat helmet and putting it on. He then flipped the goggles down. The helmet's heads-up display had already locked on to the marked area and a small green square alongside range information now illuminated it. Since he'd been assigned to work alongside the two squads below, his comms had been linked into their channel, and he could hear the sergeants issuing concise orders. His concern for now though would be getting this tank of his to a working state. He activated the tank's internal comms.

"Hershall, what's up?"

"Fucking thing won't start!"

The tank shook again, this time followed by a rattle coming from the engine compartment.

"Keep trying."

Honig ducked down into the turret and activated emergency power. It wouldn't start the engine, but it'd at least get the turret running for a short period of time. There was a short beep, and the turret controls came to life. Honig then pulled himself forward to the left of the breach and into the gunner's seat. Seconds later the tank's fire control system had linked into the squad network and the marked area appeared on the firing computer's screen. Turning the turret left, he put the reticle directly onto the green square.

"On target. Awaiting your orders, over," reported Honig.

"Hold fire, we're moving up," answered one of the sergeants.

"Received."

The tank shook again, and the engine roared to life, soon subsiding to a low hum.

"We're good!" reported Hershall.

"Excellent, hold tight."

Honig eyed the monitor. Five troops were moving up in a skirmish line, rifles raised. Apparently, whatever it was that they were seeing did not seem like much of a threat, else they likely would have remained in the trench.

Within a few minutes their sergeant radioed back. "Looks like a civy. We're pulling him back now."

56

As Honig zoomed in with the targeting computer, the men pulled a man up and out of the tall grass, one soldier holding on to each of his arms. The sergeant kept the muzzle of his rifle firmly jammed into the guy's back, while the remaining two soldiers continued to aim into the valley covering their return up the hillside. The man was soaking wet, dressed in blue jeans and a dark grey sweater. His expression looked like a mix of fear and relief. Honig pulled the main gun's aim away from the group, instead aiming at the fog obscured ground behind them. Better to make sure no one popped out of the grass down there than continue to aim at something under control.

Soon enough, the squad had pulled the man up the hill behind the trench line and pushed him face down into the ground. Two soldiers alongside the platoon medic then proceeded the strip him down, searching and scanning him for any kind of weapon or transmitter. This only took about five minutes, at which point they wrapped the man in a raincoat and called for a vehicle to pick him up. Whether he was a civilian trying to escape to the Earth Union, or some sort of Novian spy, he wouldn't be getting far. Within the next ten minutes, one of the armored personnel carriers arrived and the man was promptly thrown in the back. After the APC drove off, one of the squad sergeants radioed Honig.

"Squad 2 to CE tank, how are things looking from up there?"

Honig had been keeping an eye on the slopes below, but none the less checked one more time before answering. "All clear."

Chapter 11 - Lull

31 August 2431 – 12:00

It had gotten darker since his watch shift had ended. As an added bonus, the rain had picked up. Honig sat on a pile of olive drab supply crates, wrapped in his raincoat and watching the men of the motorized company make final adjustments to the landing field. Not that there were many to make at this point. Any areas that needed filling in had since been filled, and there wasn't much in the way of brush or small trees to clear. Those troops who had finished up were either on patrol at the field's edges or taking cover from the rain in the APCs.

Honig eyed one of the APCs. If the armed forces were going to retake the city, or even hold this hill, they were going to need a lot more in the way of men and equipment here than this. Looking over at the tree line, he watched as another squad approached out of the fog, then looked back down at the crate he was sitting on. It wasn't something that he should have to worry about anyway, unless they planned on throwing the CE Office into this fight, which was possible. Though, why would they want to? As fighting men, the CE would be sub-par at best. Best not to worry about it.

He stood up, shaking off some of the accumulated rainwater before walking toward the nearest of the three APCs. Its crew was sitting in the back with the rear doors open. All three wore dark green jump suits, with only one wearing an armored vest. The rest of their body armor lay on the seats further in.

As Honig approached, the driver looked up. "G'day."

Honig leaned up against the back of the APC. "Good day." He looked over the crew for a moment. "They don't issue you guys the full suits?"

"No, not for us," answered the driver.

"They do for the trackies though," added one of the other crewmen.

Honig chuckled when he heard the term. "Trackies" was a general term thrown around to refer to anyone driving a tracked combat vehicle, typically tanks. "Been a while since I've heard that term."

"You've served?" asked the driver.

"Armored, in the last war."

"Hey!" The driver smiled. "We have a tracky here gents!" He reached out and shook Honig's hand. "Sergeant Auger, good to meet you."

"Call me Frank."

"So, what're you doing here?"

"Civil Enforcement. Still running tanks though," said Honig.

"You're the guy in charge of that ugly thing?"

Before Honig could answer, one of the other crewmen cut in. "I thought it looked pretty good in that black and white. Sleek!"

Sergeant Auger then looked over at the crewman. "Sticks out like a bloody thumb though."

Honig raised his eyebrows, a look of amusement across his face. "At least I look good riding in it."

"Can't argue with you there." Auger reached down to the floor of the APC and brought up a heated thermos, offering it to Honig.

"No thank you, I'm good."

"You look bloody freezing."

"Eh, I've been better." A short silence followed. "So, how long have you guys been in?"

"Almost two years. Figures, just two months and I could've been outta here!"

"Now you get to stick with us!" The crewman to Auger's left slapped him on the shoulder.

"Fuck you and your infantry ass!"

The crewman laughed. "Hey now, I was smart enough to get my ass *out* of the infantry."

"But still dumb enough to get stuck here."

"Ugly bastid."

At this the four of them, including Honig, broke down laughing. Hershall then walked up awkwardly.

"Ay! Another tracky!" exclaimed Auger. His two crewmen again burst out laughing.

Hershall just stared at the group, confused. "What?"

"Not exactly a tracky," said Honig, looking over at Hershall.

"Just an officer then?"

"Specialist, actually," answered Hershall, a cold expression across his face.

"Hey now! We're just breaking your balls mate!" Auger tapped one of the seats closest to the APC's door. "Sit your special ass down and have a drink. It's awful out!" He then looked up at Honig. "You too actually, why are you just standin' there in the rain?"

Before Honig could accept the offer Hershall spoke up, looking at Honig. "Sir, Chief Eckhart has requested your presence."

"What? Everything alright?"

"Not sure."

Honig's heart sank. He turned towards the APC's crew. "Well gents, hopefully we'll meet again."

"Your boss calling for ya?"

"Yeah."

"Good luck!"

Honig gave a small wave and began to walk away with Hershall.

"You realize it won't be long before you're working alongside them, right?" said Honig.

"I suppose so."

"At a minimum you should get used to them. They're fellow armed forces."

"I know."

They walked a bit further in silence.

"Any idea what's up?" asked Honig.

"I honestly have no idea."

"Quite possibly looking to force me into retirement."

"I certainly hope not."

By now they had reached the olive drab command tent, set up by the motorized troops when they arrived. As they approached, the words "...and where the fuck is Weiss?" could distinctly be heard from the tent's interior.

Hershall knocked on the tent's flimsy front door. "Captain Honig here for you, sir."

"Come on in," said Chief Eckhart. As Hershall went to step forward Eckhart stopped him. "Just Honig, thank you."

Hershall stepped back and waved Honig in.

The tent was not particularly large, but it was well lit and air conditioned so that it was not nearly so humid inside. The tent clearly was not intended for long term use, as there was only a minimal assortment of maps and computer equipment set up. One of the motorized company's communications officers sat in front of one of the computers. Further back, the company lieutenant was leaning against a beam on the back wall. In the center a large table had been set up, at which Chief Eckhart and a young, charismatic looking soldier sat.

"Captain Honig!" The young soldier stood up and reached out his hand. "Or perhaps Colonel Honig of 2nd Armored suits you better?"

Honig shook the young soldier's hand, a suspicious expression across his face. "Recruitment officer?"

"Yes sir! Sergeant Struble's my name." The soldier sat back down, gesturing to Honig to take a seat.

Honig took the seat. "It has been a little while since I've been referred to by that title." Honig turned to Eckhart. "What's this about?"

Before Eckhart could speak, the young sergeant answered, "Given the current situation we have a distinct lack of experienced personnel. We'd like to offer you an opportunity to rejoin the service."

"You really want some old guy like me running tanks again?"

"Most of the men have not seen actual combat yet, you have. It'll be good to have a cool head in the lead."

"In the lead?"

"We're looking to grant you your prior rank of Colonel. You won't be going in as a grunt again."

Honig stared back blankly.

"Thirty confirmed armored kills. Few people can tout that kind of record."

"Thirty-two. I see they still haven't corrected that," muttered Honig. He leaned forward, massaging his temples. "What are the details?"

"As you are a special case sir, you can expect at least double the benefits for your-"

"No. What would be my assignment? What unit would I be running with?"

"We're looking to assign you to an armored platoon. For your first few operations you'll be functioning as the platoon leader. Once you are re-acclimated, you'll be put in charge of said platoon. If things go well, there are company command positions that we are looking to fill."

"Honig," Eckhart cut in. "Despite what it sounds like this is in fact optional. You've done your service."

Honig leaned back in his chair, thinking. He'd served in the previous war, successfully. Multiple tours in fact. When his time came to retire, he was offered a position as an instructor for the armored corps, but he declined, instead having elected to take up a job on this backwater world where he could live out his days. He looked down at his hands. Perhaps it was time again. "It's either me or someone else." He exhaled, then looked up at Struble. "Sign me up. I'm ready to go."

Struble promptly pulled out a spread of re-enlistment papers and handed a pen to Honig. The first papers covered the contract between him and the armed forces, specifically his "special case", taking on his prior rank immediately upon re-enlistment and recognizing that he was substantially older than the typical recruit. The second group of pages covered medical history, short and to the point. Despite having some augmentations that would normally disqualify Honig from regular service, the first page covering the "special case" negated this. He'd be good to go regardless of his medical state. Last but not least were papers titled with K/MIA, in case of Killed or Missing in Action. Honig pushed these aside. "No need."

Struble looked at him. "Are you sure?"

Honig had already thought it through. He had no family, and if there was anything left of his stuff when the war ended, there was no need to dump it on his friends. "Yes."

At this, Struble neatened up the stack of papers and said, "Welcome back to the Earth Union Armed Forces."

The motorized company lieutenant then stepped forward and shook Honig's hand. "I suggest you get some sleep. We'll be heading out soon."

Chapter 12 – LZ North

31 August 2431 – 22:00

They had been driving north along the dirt road for about twenty minutes now. In an effort to minimize their presence, the driver was making use of his night vision. No headlights, nor the interior lights of the vehicle were activated, leaving Honig in total darkness.

Eight hours before, he had made his final goodbyes to Shepard, Hershall, and a few other members of the department. The general consensus was that the Civil Enforcement office would be seeing combat, albeit in a support role. They would be tasked with defending rear areas and providing logistical support where possible. Depending on how long this conflict lasted, most CE personnel would eventually be integrated into the regular armed forces. The exact timeline for that was still open for debate.

The car hit a bump, jarring Honig back awake. Prior to this mess, these logging roads were made to assist in scientific research and make way for the eventual expansion of living space in this area. Echelon was close to being given to go ahead for the construction of suburban type neighborhoods, as local flora and fauna was proving safe enough to permit less concentrated settlement. Now, said roads were proving extremely convenient for the efficient movement of armed forces.

"How long until we get there?"

"Not much longer. Maybe ten minutes," answered the driver. "If I may make a suggestion: get your helmet set up before we get there. Total blackout."

"Of course." Honig searched around in the darkness, eventually getting a grip on his helmet.

Spinning it around in his hands he oriented it as best he could and pulled it on. Opening the panel on his left gauntlet, he activated his helmet's night vision. He squinted for a moment at the sudden brightness of his now illuminated heads-up display before focusing on the cab, then out the windows. There was an armored car ahead of them as well as behind. Both were two seaters, designed for light reconnaissance. The vehicle in which Honig rode was an extended version, featuring four seats and a top hatch. Two infantrymen sat in the back. One appeared to be asleep. The other was far more alert. Suddenly, the car shook as something massive flew low overhead.

"One of ours," reported the driver. "Nothin' to worry about."

Peering up through the windshield, Honig could see the glow of the ship's thrusters as it disappeared behind the tree line. It had been a long time, but they appeared to be the right configuration: four bright rectangles, one on each corner. Novian drop ships typically had round thrusters, or at least they used to.

It wasn't long before they reached the staging ground. Like the area the CE had set up in, it was another naturally formed field, with minor clearing around the edges. Unlike that area, this landing field was packed with equipment. Along the back edge thirteen or so main battle tanks were lined up, their crews abuzz around them. Everywhere else, at least a company of infantry was roving about, either moving off field or towards armored personnel carriers on the opposite side.

In the center of the field the dropship that had passed over them earlier hovered a few feet off the ground, forty men piling out the back of it. Earth Union drop ships were massive vehicles, built in a blocky, horizontal 'U' shape. The ship's bridge was located at the bottom of the 'U', with the two passenger compartments branching off either side. A large crane setup was located in the center behind the ship's bridge, and typically carried some sort of armored vehicle to accompany the infantry. This was a combat drop, with the ship hovering a meter above the ground and unloading its passengers before taking off as quickly as possible, revealing the tank that had moments before been locked in between the two passenger compartments. As the men rushed off to the edge of the field, the tank turned around and moved to join the rest of the line.

Honig's vehicle turned left, proceeding to the back edge of the landing zone. As they did this, they passed a group of five men, all carrying large communications arrays on their backs. Drone operators by the look of them.

70

Three of them were already directing their fleets of spy craft, as the fourth tossed a handful of bug-sized drones into the air. The fifth appeared to be putting together something larger, but Honig couldn't get a good look at it in time. At the back of the field there was a soldier waiting for them. He saluted as Honig got out of the armored car.

"Colonel Honig! Welcome to 4th Armored. If you could please follow me, sir."

Before doing so, Honig turned to the driver and shook his hand. "Thank you much. Stay safe out there."

"My pleasure, sir." The driver saluted and got back into his vehicle.

Honig then turned back around and followed the soldier. Behind the field there were a few tents set up. The private waved Honig into the closest one, pulling the tent flap aside for him. The interior was dimly lit with a single red bulb in each corner. Strewn along the tent's walls were equipment crates, on top of which sat a sergeant and a medic, both in full combat gear minus their helmets. The sergeant stood up and faced Honig.

"Colonel Honig?"

"That's me."

"I am Sergeant Karun. I'll be assisting with your gear." He then gestured to the medic. "This is Staff Sergeant Müller. He'll be performing a brief medical examination while we get you set up."

The Staff Sergeant then stood up. "Sir."

Honig looked at the both of them. "What first?"

"Down to your boxers. Karun will get your suit ready," answered Müller.

Honig began unclipping the various armor plates of his gear, starting with the gauntlets before moving to his breastplate and leg armor. As he did this, Karun pulled an AC Suit out of one of the crates on the floor. The "Alternative Combat Suit" was a skintight undergarment, packed with thousands of expanding and contracting strands meant to mimic muscle. It was standard issue in the Earth Union Armed Forces, providing increased strength to the user, removing sweat, and regulating the user's temperature through a complex series of ducts. It was also airtight, providing a full seal when combined with standard issue combat helmets.

As Honig stripped down, Müller brought out a computer tablet and began scrolling through its menus. "Let me see if our records are correct." He opened Frank Honig's file. "Muscle reinforcement sheets installed in both calves. Same thing in the thighs, correct?"

"Yes." Honig had finished removing his armor plates and was now pulling off his battle dress uniform.

"When were they last checked on, and have you had any issues with them?"

"Four months ago, no issues."

Müller scrolled down to another menu. "A mechanical back re-structuring. How's that holding up?"

"Just fine."

"Is there a reason that you elected to go with mechanical upgrades over rejuvenate treatments?"

"Couldn't afford it." It was a lie, but Honig wasn't in the mood to explain.

Müller raised an eyebrow. "Ok then." He scrolled down one more time. "But you did get a regenerative done for your vitals. Those holding up alright?"

"Yes." Honig was down to his boxers and was shivering in the cold.

Karun moved forward to start getting Honig into the AC suit, but Müller stopped him.

"One more thing…" Müller pulled out a hand scanner and proceeded to run it past all the areas where Honig had augmentations installed. Once finished, he turned it off and re-attached it to his gear. "You look good to go. But just a heads up, if any of those reinforcement sheets go, we're not going to be able to repair them in the field. That's it."

Honig nodded.

"Aight, gear up." Müller picked up his helmet and donned it. "Good luck, sir." He saluted, then exited the tent.

The AC suit had a "zipper" of sorts running from the right side of the hip to the left, then up to the left collar bone. Honig slid his legs into the suit first. As he did so, it tightened around his body, making numerous tiny shifts to better adapt to his shape. Next, he slid his arms into the sleeves, in the process bringing the torso part of the suit up onto his shoulders. Karun then stepped forward and closed the front flap, sealing it. Air hissed up from the collar past Honig's ears as it began pressing out air pockets.

"The more you move around the better adjusted the suit will be. Once you have the rest of your gear on. I'd recommend taking a short walk around the field. That should get everything to where it needs to be."

Next, Karun pulled out the external layer of Honig's gear, a thick, dark grey, fireproof suit. Like the AC suit, it featured reinforced panels integrated into the elbows, shoulders, knees, and torso. The boots were a part of the suit, technically removable though it wasn't an easy process. While it did not provide the same ballistic protection of infantry armor, it permitted easier movement and increased thermal protection, similar to fireman's gear. In other words, it was optimized for what it was designed to do: protect tank crews. This did not take long to put on.

"This thing come with gloves?"

"Yes." Karun handed Honig a set of gloves. "Also, one more thing." He pulled out a set of patches, colonel markings. "Your other markings did not arrive in time. We don't have a name tag for you either. We'll be making arrangements to get that in."

As Honig attached the two patches to Velcro panels on his chest and right shoulder, Karun pulled out the last piece of the ensemble, a brand-new tanker helmet. Honig took it and looked it over. Externally, it looked like a black, stripped down infantry helmet. The metal neck guards had been replaced with flexible Kevlar panels and smaller audio modules had been put in place to reduce the helmet's width.

Pulling it on, Honig asked, "They still using the EZ Breath systems on these things?"

"From what I understand they improved them in the last few years. Not sure on the specifics how, but it has made a difference."

Honig took a few deep breaths. Aside from the plastic scent of filtered air there was no difference between now and breathing with the helmet off. "That it has." He slid his hands along the bottom rim of the helmet until he found the release latches. Upon pressing them in there was a brief hiss as the air seal disengaged, and he pulled it off. "Looks like everything fits. Where's my crew?"

"I'll have to check with the flight controller, but they'll be arriving in their, or rather, your tank. Number 401, a TAV27. They might be on the ground already. If you're all set, we can check it out right now."

"Yes, let's go."

Karun nodded, then put on his helmet and activated his night vision before heading for the door. Honig did the same and proceeded to move forward. The first few steps were stiff, with the AC suit freezing up and making rapid re-adjustments. By the time he'd reached the tent's exit his movement had smoothed out. Before exiting, he turned and looked at the pile of his old CE gear laying on the floor. He shook his head and then stepped out.

There were at least three more tanks in the line at the back of the field now, and another dropship was just coming in to drop off its passengers. Behind the line of tanks, a self-propelled anti-aircraft gun drove along slowly. It was a new model that Honig didn't recognize, utilizing the same hull as the TAV27 Main Battle Tank but with a quad-barreled anti-aircraft gun mounted in place of the standard MBT turret.

"Over here, sir!" shouted Karun over the rumble of engines and aircraft thrusters. He was about ten meters away next to what Honig assumed was the communications tent. Karun opened the tent flap and leaned in.

"Yo, Mac! 401 arrive yet?"

"Tank?" an unseen voice from inside asked.

"Yeah."

"Arrived a few minutes ago, second or third one in from the end."

"Thank you, sir!" Karun waved then stepped back, turning to Honig. "Right this way."

Moving their way through a flurry of men and equipment they reached the tank line, eventually finding the one they were looking for. As they approached the crew could be seen outside of it, pulling protective covers off, checking optics, and making sure everything was locked down. This pleased Honig. Theoretically, tanks that arrived via combat drop were battle ready, though it never hurt to double check everything when circumstance permitted.

"401!" shouted Karun.

One of the three crewmen looked up, then tapped the shoulder of the man next to him. All three then jumped down. Seeing Honig's colonel patches, they stood at attention and saluted. Except for their name tags and rank markings, the three of them looked identical in their full suits.

"Colonel Honig, this is your crew. Sergeant Unger, Specialist Linski, and Private First Class KP403."

Honig looked over KP403 then turned to Karun. "A clone on my crew? Is it at least stable?"

"Yes, he is, sir."

Honig turned back to KP403. "What should I call you KP403?"

"You can call me Kip, sir."

"Creative. Good to meet you all." Honig stepped forward and shook their hands. "What's our status?"

"Fully loaded and ready to go. Drop was successful, no damage to report so far, sir," answered Sergeant Unger.

"Excellent. What's the battle plan?"

"I'll be happy to brief you, sir."

Chapter 13 – One Minute to Midnight

31 August 2431 – 23:59

Honig's control screen and heads-up display flickered dully, presumably a result of another EMP burst saturating the area. This constant flickering was giving him a headache. Out of habit, he brought his gloved left hand up to massage his temples, only to remember that he was wearing a full helmet and couldn't. Instead, he ran his fingers along the smooth edge of his helmet's left side hearing module.

The tank's interior was illuminated by a series of red lights, with all the controls glowing a dim green. In the few places where there weren't buttons or control screens the walls were painted a semi-gloss white, the standard color for vehicle interiors. The layout was, for the most part, very similar to the older T26 that Honig used in the CE. The few changes there were in the control layouts were trivial, though annoying at times when he went to try and reach for a once-familiar switch. Returning his focus to his command screen, he reviewed the plan one more time.

Honig's platoon would be taking up the spearhead, the lead element of the assault. When the time came, each armored unit would move into their assigned positions within the tree line at the edge of the valley, spread out to maximize their effective firepower and reduce vulnerability to enemy artillery and airstrikes. For the advance, armored-infantry units would accompany the tanks, moving up just behind until contact with the enemy. The anti-aircraft sections and point defense systems would remain behind on the hill, providing supporting fire for the duration of the advance. Overall, the battle plan seemed solid, except for the fact that they had no clue where Novus was, what Novus had, or even if the Novians were on the opposite side of the valley.

"Looks good," said Honig.

"Happy to hear that, sir," answered Unger. He was sitting in the gunner's position, just ahead of Honig.

Honig leaned back a little in his seat, feeling the back of his fireproof suit compress. "I must inquire, what happened to your previous commander?"

Unger turned to the right a bit. "Freak accident, really. His hand got caught between a shell container and a wall in zero g. He was lucky to not have lost it."

"Geez. How long ago did that happen?"

"Just over a week ago. Funny that we received word of the war the next day."

"You guys found out about this a week ago?"

"Yeah, why?"

"Down here we found out two days ago." Honig thought about it for a moment. "I guess it explains how you guys managed to mobilize so quickly."

"We'd actually been put on alert a few days before that. Thought it was a drill at the time."

"It always starts like that." They sat in silence for a minute before Honig spoke up again. "So, where you from?"

"What?"

"Where are you from?" repeated Honig more slowly.

"Earth, North American Coalition. You?"

"Earth born, though I spent most of my early years on Mars."

"Mars? You're lucky. No one gets to go there."

"My adoptive family was from there."

"Wow. So, what's it like?"

"Good living, low taxes. Back when I was growing up there still weren't a lot of trees, though. Really there still aren't. Been a little while since I've lived there."

"I never would have left. My family's lives in New York, mid-level. We didn't see much in the way of trees either."

"That is one thing I have yet to see, one of those super cities."

"So, it's true that there are none on Mars?"

"Yeah. Buildings were never very tall on Mars. Really no need to."

"Don't start. The cities suck."

"Hm?"

"When it rains all the shit from the upper levels washes into the lower levels," answered Unger.

"You'd need one heck of an umbrella."

"Trust me, we have them."

Honig then turned to the clone. "So, where'd they make you?"

"Orbital Station 16 around Earth, Gestator 4."

"And were you made for this or just re-purposed?"

"Bred for battle, sir." A hint of pride almost seemed to enter its voice.

"When did they start training you?"

"Socialization until year 10 equivalent, all training and education after that point." The clone was performing his final checks on the tank's communications systems and hadn't skipped a beat.

"Interesting." Honig didn't like the idea of a manufactured *thing* potentially outmatching him in proficiency. It'd been a long time since he'd encountered clone troops. The rumor he'd heard was that the newest generation of them were hyper intelligent and physically superior to natural humans. It was a legitimate question as to how the Earth Union intended to keep them under control. Turning back to Unger, he asked, "Is it just me or does this whole plan seem rushed?"

"It is. Word is that Earth ordered the armed forces to attack on all fronts. Like, immediately."

"Really? Where'd you hear that?"

"Overheard one of the pilots talking. Supposedly, the fleet wanted to regroup before moving forward with anything, but obviously that didn't happen."

"Huh."

Honig's thoughts were then interrupted by a radio transmission from the armored company commander. "Command to all platoons, prepare to move into your designated positions, over."

"Alright," started Honig. "Let's do this, boys."

The order appeared on Honig's command screen and he pressed a key indicating that he had received it and was ready. He then activated the tank's view system, a series of cameras on the top of the turret that when linked with Honig's heads-up display permitted him to look around seamlessly. To the left, he could see the crew of the next tank over scrambling to get in. They really should have already been on board. On the right side were the marine armored platoons, already set to go. Up front, one of the company lieutenants had exited his tank and was on foot with two reflective batons, trying to guide the platoons out one at a time.

Honig's platoon was the third out. First the platoon leader, 4-0, moved forward, immediately followed by Honig, 401, taking up his left side. 402 and 403 then took up the right side. Once across the field, the platoon proceeded to enter the woods the same way the previous two platoons did. With the low brush having already been crushed down this initial move was easy, at least until it was time to break off from the main route. Turning to face east, the platoon slowed down to a walking pace. Better to drive carefully than risk getting stuck. Even with some of the best night vision systems available, seeing through the maze of black trees and patches of brush was difficult at best. Add in the wet soil and it was a perfect recipe for mishaps. Luck seemed to be on their side though, and they'd soon reached their assigned waypoint, just within the tree line overlooking the valley below.

Honig pressed a key on his command screen notifying the rest of his platoon that he was all set. The platoon leader and the other two tanks then checked in with the same status. From here, Honig could just barely see the valley through the gaps in the trees. At least he'd have something to look at until it was time to go.

Chapter 14 – The End

1 September 2431 – 05:00

The cloud layer had thinned substantially, and for the first time in weeks yellow light illuminated the valley from the rising sun. The fog had cleared, leaving only the rising mist between the battlegroup and the other side of the valley. The dew on the fields below glinted gold in the light.

The advance had been delayed, having originally been set to start at least three hours before. Command had ordered the halt after having received "new intel", but nothing came of it since. There were those who thought that perhaps it was all a mistake, and that the war wasn't going to happen. That of course was too good to be true. The order to advance had finally come and all units were now exiting the tree line. Initially, progress was slow as they maintained the speeds that had successfully gotten them through the thick woods. As they entered open ground, they increased their speed. Each armored platoon was moving up in a loose wedge with a mechanized platoon moving up a hundred meters behind. Just ahead of and spread out among the formations tracked drones zoomed along.

Eyeing the opposite side of the valley, Honig switched to thermal, then back to regular. Nothing was showing up on either.

"Kip, you see anything?"

"Negative."

An aerial combat drone then flew overhead. As it reached the halfway point over the valley, a missile suddenly shot up from the horizon and blasted one of its wings off, sending it spinning down into the opposite slope.

"All units, we have contact on the hill," reported the platoon leader.

Honig again switched to thermal, but it didn't appear to be working properly. Even the burning wreckage of the drone didn't light up. Seconds later, tank 403 came over the comms asking if anyone else was experiencing anomalies with their optics.

"401 here, same issue, over," reported Honig. Squinting at his heads-up display, he again switched it back to normal, just in time to see multiple bright flashes emanate from opposite side of the valley.

"Incoming fire!"

The tank shook as its reactive armor system activated and successfully deflected the first projectile with a concentrated blast of chaff.

"Sergeant, fire at will!"

"Targeting computer can't lock on! Switching to manual."

The platoon leader's voice then came in over the comms. "All units, continue the advance!"

The engine roared as the tank jolted forward, rocking as a nearby explosion shook the hull. Honig switched back to thermal and started diagnostics, but there were no errors to report.

"403 here, we've been hit! I think we're good..."

Looking right, Honig could see that tank 403 had taken a hit to its side skirts. As a result, a shower of sparks shot out as the tracks ground against the bent armor plates. One of the APCs coming up behind had taken a hit as well, sliding to a halt as fire began to pour out of every crevice. Its rear door then slammed down, and infantrymen began stumbling out, covered in burning fuel.

Honig's tank shook as the main gun fired. As the gun's action slammed back a spent shell was kicked along a rail leading to an ejection port near the back of the turret. A new shell was then lifted up from storage and slammed forward into the breach with a large mechanical plunger. As soon as the breach clicked shut the loading status displays switched to green, indicating that the gun was again ready to fire.

From the non-thermal cameras, silhouettes of enemy vehicles were now visible on the hillside, the enemy's guns having pushed aside the piles of brush that once concealed them. The command interface then turned red with the words "Incoming Artillery Fire" across the top in bold black print. As it did this, the sky lit up with strings of anti-aircraft fire, high intensity lasers, and explosions as the point defense systems on the hill behind them activated. However, as effective as these systems were, shells from the incoming barrage soon began to slip through, kicking up massive black clouds of dirt and debris as they exploded just above the ground. As the closest blast cleared, the hill suddenly lit up with numerous large heat signatures, most appearing to be Novian main battle tanks.

"Must've been some sort of cloak…" mumbled Honig, wide-eyed.

"Target locks acquired!" reported Sergeant Unger.

The ground leveled out as they entered the bottom of the valley at high speed, looking up at the enemy. Now that they could see what they were dealing with, it was brutally clear that they were at a disadvantage.

"402 here, driver's dead, we're still fighting, though."

Honig's tank fired again. The shell traveled to its target as intended, only to ricochet off its hull and detonate further up the hill. The enemy tank then fired back. This time, the reactive armor did not stop the shot. The impact was similar to getting hit in the head with a sledgehammer. Every electronic system on board flickered. Honig looked around, waiting for his helmet's hearing modules to recover.

"Is everybody alright?" he shouted.

"We're good!"

They fired back, and this time their shot met its mark, blasting a hole in the front of the enemy's turret. There must have been some damage to its barrel as well, as it proceeded to detonate when it attempted to fire back.

Just as Sergeant Unger started to cheer. they received another hit. The impact slammed their front-left corner, causing the tank to pull left hard before grinding to a halt.

"Front drive wheel gone! I'll see what I can do…" reported Linski.

Before Honig could report their status, the platoon leader came in over the comms. "Halt advance, supporting fire inbound."

"Fuck!" Honig keyed his mic. "401, we're disabled, still firing!"

"Heads up 401, you're right at the edge of the target area."

Unger swung the turret right and began firing the coaxial at some infantry who had appeared up the hill. Seconds later some sort of shoulder fired rocket ricocheted off the top of the turret. The supporting fire, in the form of a missile barrage, then slammed down. The next two minutes sounded like a train driving through the crew compartment as missile after missile exploded nearby. Visibility, even with the thermal, was reduced to near zero as waves of soil and plant matter were kicked up into a storm. The camera system was then sheared off entirely as a missile slammed down into the ground just feet away from the tank's right side.

"Sergeant! Are the gun sights still intact?"

"Yes, sir!"

The hull was rocked one more time as another missile exploded nearby, then the rumbling stopped. Honig stood up from his seat, looking through the now scratched and soiled view ports of the cupola. The waves of dirt were now replaced with a thick haze of white smoke through which he could only see ten, maybe fifteen meters away. Until it cleared, he wouldn't be very useful.

"Sir, hostiles north-east up the hill!"

"If you can see them, shoot them. I can't see shit from here."

Rather than replying, Unger just opened fire with the coaxial.

"Kip," started Honig. "Figure out our exact coordinates and relay them and our status to the rest of the platoon."

"Affirmative." The clone appeared unfazed, and almost immediately began sending the message.

Suddenly the entire interior of the turret flashed white. As Honig fell back into his seat from the impact, a spray of fluid spattered across his lenses. Looking right and seeing the body of Kip slumped backward with a significant chunk of his belly missing, Honig realized what had happened.

"Kip!" Honig began climbing over what was left of auto loading system, but his heads-up display confirmed his theory before he could get to him.

"What the fuck just happened!?" shouted Unger.

"We've been hit. Kip's dead!" The tank's computer system was showing Kip's vitals as having completely ceased.

"Fuck! Kip!" Unger's voice nearly cracked.

Honig attempted to wipe the blood off his goggles but only managed to smear it. Pulling himself back to his seat, he looked over the damage. While the blast had just missed the breach, the auto loading system had been destroyed and was now very much in the way. It would be possible to pull it back, but it would take time.

"Sergeant!"

Unger was holding the sides of his helmet and rocking forward and backwards.

"Sergeant Unger, focus! We have one shot left, make it count!"

"Fuck!" Unger put his hands back on the controls and turned the turret right, beginning to aim.

As Unger did this, Honig keyed his mic. "401 here, we've taken casualties and are in need of assistance, over!"

"4-0 to 401, stay put, we have guys coming to get you!" answered the platoon leader.

As Unger fired the main gun its breach slammed back into the loading plunger, snapping it. The only half ejected shell was then pinched as the breach attempted to shut automatically. Meanwhile, all the loading indicators in the turret flashed yellow with more errors than could fit on the screens. Brushing broken pieces of metal off his thigh, Honig stood back up to look out of the cupola, just in time to see another shot coming towards them.

Like the previous one, the interior of the turret was momentarily illuminated by a white flash, only this time the damage was far worse. The shot penetrated just below the gun mantlet, deflecting up off the turret ring and into the underside of the breach, causing it to explode and sending shards of metal flying throughout the compartment.

Honig screamed as something sharp penetrated his gut and he fell into his seat attempting to cover the wound. Looking down at his gloves he saw blood. Moaning, he turned off the message in his helmet indicating that his suit had been punctured. He didn't need the reminder. He was then alerted by the fact that the interior of the turret was on fire.

Almost immediately, the interior fire suppression system activated, and the turret was filled with white sudsy foam. As quickly as it had appeared, it then melted away leaving only an oily film over everything. Before Honig could even breathe a sigh of relief, the fire re-kindled in the front of the turret.

"Shit! Unger!" Wincing in pain Honig began moving forward towards Unger who was leaning left against the wall, fire forming around his right side.

Grabbing hold of Unger's shoulder, Honig shook him. He was unresponsive, but according to the computer he was still alive. As Honig got into position to pull Unger out, a hydraulic line underneath the destroyed breach burst, igniting almost immediately and covering both of them in burning liquid.

Honig cursed loudly, not that it would help. Though he was protected from the flames for now, the heat was quickly beginning to penetrate the compressed portions of his suit. Sliding his arms under Unger's armpits he pulled as hard as he could. Even with the augmented strength of the suit he could feel the muscles in his back seize up. Despite this, within a minute he had managed to pull Unger up out of the gunner's seat to just forward of the cupola. It was now that the heat of the fire began to penetrate his gloves.

Letting go of Unger, he punched open the hatch with both of his fists. With the introduction of fresh air into the cabin, fire quickly enveloped the entirety of the turret's interior. None the less, Honig reached back down and grabbed the sergeant under both arms.

"Ahhhhhh!" The shout was a mixture of adrenaline and pain as he pushed Unger's torso up through the hatch. With another push, gravity took over and Unger's body fell off the left side of the turret's exterior. Now it was Honig's turn. Standing up, he pulled himself up and out of the hatch. Once out, he rolled off the left side of the turret, slamming down onto the tank's fender before falling into a blast crater in the ground next to Unger.

Both of their suits were burned black, pieces of Kevlar and fabric flaking off in the breeze. Honig hadn't noticed earlier, but the lower portion of Unger's right arm had been blasted off, the wound thoroughly cauterized by a mix of fire and melted plastic. Unger was still breathing though, and that was what mattered.

Rolling over on his back Honig looked at his own hands. The thick gloves were thoroughly burnt, and wisps of smoke emanated from them. He attempted to sit up, but the entirety of his back was in spasm and he was unable to. Instead, he began fumbling at his faceplate, searching with numb fingers for what was left of the removal latches. Within a few minutes he managed to pull it off, melted rubber sticking to his ill-shaven cheeks. The entirety of him smelled like a mix of burnt meat and plastic. It was no worse than the stench of the smoking ground around him.

Throwing his faceplate aside, he lay his head back down on the ground, his helmet pressing into the dirt.

Staring up into the light grey sky, he watched as the smoke disappeared into the heavens. By this point even his legs refused to move. They, like his back, had locked up and something had snapped in his right calf, though it didn't really matter now. He would wait this one out. A few minutes to rest perhaps. Finally.

Epilogue – No Rest for the Wicked

1 September 2431 – 19:32

Novian Forward Medical Post – Reppertum Valley, Eastern Side, Echelon

"Sir, we've got another one coming in. Priority."

"Thank you, Lieutenant."

Wounded had been coming in all day, and there seemed to be no sign of it stopping. Dr. Cohen ran his left hand across his forehead, trying to stave off an impending headache. Standing up from his chair, he picked up his blood-stained coat and once again threw it on. Even the Novian seal on the right breast pocket was spattered.

"What's it look like?"

"Burn injuries, possible lacerations to the abdomen."

Dr. Cohen looked at the Lieutenant. They'd had vehicle crews coming in all day with such injuries.

"You better come see," continued the Lieutenant.

Cohen nodded and grabbed his PDA, a hand-held tablet that could synchronize with nearby medical equipment and give him a rapid overview of a patient's status. Stepping into the hallway, the lieutenant led him to the front entrance, where two infantrymen and a medic were pushing a man in on a gurney. The first thing Cohen noticed was the man's uniform, an Earth Union tanker.

"You serious?"

"Trust me doc," answered the field medic, and he gently pulled the man's helmet off, revealing a head of white hair and wrinkled skin.

"Jesus!" The man on the gurney looked old enough to be Cohen's grandfather. "Alright, let's go."

As the two infantrymen resumed pushing, the medic began opening the patient's outer suit, ripping open melted zippers and pulling armor plates aside.

"AC suit's still intact, at least on the torso," reported the medic. Pulling aside the lower section of the chest armor he then cursed aloud. "Scratch that." There was a two-inch-long piece of shrapnel sticking out of the suit's belly section. As far as they could tell, the suit had already constricted around the wound and was currently holding the metal in place.

"Somebody get me a calibrator."

"Already on it," answered a nurse, handing the tool to Cohen.

Cohen handed two cables to the field medic who then plugged them into sockets on the front of the AC suit's right shoulder. Remarkably, they were still intact. As

Cohen synchronized his tablet with the calibrator, they entered an operating room, where two nurses had already set up the monitoring equipment and tools they'd need. Overhead a variety of automated apparatus hung, ready to go.

"Thank you much. We're set here," said Cohen, looking at the two infantrymen.

"Apologies, sir, but one of them should stand by. He's still technically an enemy combatant," interrupted the medic, gesturing towards the old man on the gurney.

"Certainly," answered Cohen.

"Nowak, hang out 'till an MP gets here."

"You got it," answered Nowak as he leaned up against the back wall, his rifle hanging from its sling.

The medic and the other soldier then left, leaving Cohen to his work. He turned back around where he was surprised to see the old man looking up at him with sad, pale blue eyes. Cohen walked up to the gurney, looking down at him.

"Hey, can you hear me? Speak English?" There was no reply. "Sprechen Sie Deutsch? Was ist dein Sprach?" Cohen's German wasn't so good, but it was worth a shot.

Looking back at his tablet, Cohen could see that the AC suit's sensors on the hands and lower legs had completely burned out, with indications of potential breeches on the right forearm alongside the obvious puncture in the belly. The suit had in fact stabilized the belly wound and reported only a minimal amount of bleeding.

"Do us a favor and stay still, alright?"

Two nurses stood by ready to hold the man down if need be, while the rest of them began cutting the outer layers and pulling them off where they could. The gloves and forearms of the outer suit practically disintegrated as nurses pulled them away, attempting to brush aside ashes. As the AC suit had reported, the interior arm and hand sections were completely burned, appearing to have melted on to the man's limbs.

"Alright, put him under."

Another nurse came out with a breathing mask and put it over the man's face. All the while, the man stared up at Cohen, his eyes slowly closing. Within moments he was unconscious, and Cohen turned to one of the nurses.

"Get Doctor Levy and a saw. We're also going to need a skin gun."

Field Medic

10 May 2433 – South of Reppertum, Echelon

Earth Union Field Medic Sergeant Johansson looked up at the dark smoky sky from his foxhole as the ground rumbled with the impact of another artillery shell. The sound was a near constant now, as it had been for the last two days.

His head swung right as a burst of rifle fire echoed across the charred ground. It wasn't near him, at least not close enough to be of immediate concern. The fighting had since razed the forest in this area and for the most part only burnt ground remained. To top it off, any advantage there would have been in visual range had since been taken away by the smoke. He looked back down at the man he was working on.

Despite Johansson's best efforts, the soldier's vitals had ceased. It was a shame. This was a young one. Pulling out a bright red electronic tag, he activated its integrated transmitter and stuck it to the front of the soldier's helmet. The tag would both identify him as dead to the other medics and assist in corpse retrieval when the time came.

Another artillery shell rocked the ground, this time closer by. Looking down at his Emergency Location System he saw two beacons activate, presumably where the shell had landed. His initial instinct was to attempt to radio the two wounded, but upon bringing his right hand up to the side of his helmet he was reminded of the damaged state of his comms. Looking up, he mentally charted a path through the rough terrain. He'd have to stay low, but he could make it.

Pulling himself up and out of the hole he ran forward, staying as low as possible and periodically checking the ELS. 25 meters, 20 meters, 18. He ducked into a ditch momentarily and looking over his ELS display realized that one of the two beacons was showing no pulse, KIA. The other beacon was slowing, but still very much alive. He could make it in time. Raising his head slightly and seeing that the way was clear, he brought forth another burst of energy, throwing himself forward over the rocks, over another hill, and finally into the blast crater.

The two casualties of the blast were immediately visible. One was clearly closer to the initial impact than the other, as he had been nearly cut in half. The other man to his right was still transmitting life signs. He'd been hit hard, but from here at least he appeared to be externally intact.

Throwing his rifle aside, Johansson got down on his knees next to the still living soldier, pulling protective covers off of the suit's medical access ports and hooking his suit into them. Through these ports he'd be able to see the downed soldier's full vitals, as well as administer tranquilizers and boosters as necessary. Just as he was about to do this, he looked up and froze.

Five Novian troops now stood above him, their rifles aimed at him. Sergeant Johansson considered for a moment what the bullets would feel like, the few that'd be stopped by his torso armor, then the many more that would tear through the steel collar and his thinly plated arms. He looked at each of them, then up into the sky. Nothing more than charred black clouds overhead. He wanted to see blue. Tiny white puffs of cloud in a great blue expanse, but there was none of that here.

Having not yet been shot, Johansson looked away from the sky back to the troops above him. They had lowered their weapons, and the leader was signaling his men forward. Within moments, three of them had formed a defensive circle around him. The leader and his corporal had gotten down next to Johansson and the wounded man on the ground, accessing their own medical tools. At this Johansson took a deep breath and got back to work.

Soon the three of them had stabilized the wounded's vitals. He would live.

Postmortem

1 March 2435 – South Quayage, Echelon

Elias looked over the massive dry docks positioned along the rocky water line. There was a break in the cloud cover along the horizon, a rare moment when the setting sun shone through brilliantly, coloring the usually silver sky gold. The light reflected calmly off the rusting beams that held up the crumbling walls of the dry docks, nearly fifty feet high. Around them and in the black sea abandoned equipment lay, some destroyed, other pieces merely neglected and left to the elements.

Elias coughed into his sleeve and sniffed. Though the snow had melted, the air had yet to let go of its winter chill. Flipping up the collar of his jacket, he shivered in the breeze. The jacket was a dirty, olive drab thing that he'd pulled from a ruined barracks block, and it wasn't meant for this weather. "For dry, warm environments," it said on the tag.

He picked up his duffel bag and began the walk down to the base of the dry dock. It was surreal how much equipment was down here, much of it appearing to have literally just been left in place mid-operation. Tractors, trucks, command cars, and anything else one could think of. Even the offices surrounding the dry docks had been left almost fully stocked - not that that their contents were useful. It was mostly paperwork and staples that they contained. Elias did find a stash of candy bars from Earth, though. Totally made the search worth it.

As he walked by one of the dark green tractors he stopped to kick at its tire. Come spring, his childhood aspirations of owning a dozen or so vehicles could quite easily come to fruition. For now, more realistic goals, like actually surviving, would have to be focused on. Not that survival was *that* hard. Among the literal piles of abandoned equipment there was no shortage of sealed military food rations. They'd be good near indefinitely provided the ration packs could be found in time and protected from the weather. Looking away from the tractor, he continued his walk to the base of the wall. Upon reaching it he pushed open a heavy rusting door, revealing the dry dock's dark interior. About 40 feet in the crew had started a campfire on the concrete, its flickering light only barely reaching the far wall.

"Elias! Certainly took you long enough."

"Nice to see you too Frank!" Elias responded to the old man sitting by the fire. There were four of them there, forming a tight circle around the flames.

Frank, by far the oldest among them, sat in the middle on an old office chair they'd pulled from one of the abandoned buildings. To his left sat Mikey, a big man about the same age as Elias. To Frank's right sat Allyson and Noam. After the armed forces disappeared four months ago, Frank and Mikey had met here at the dry docks, soon after beginning their search of the countryside for any signs
104

of life. Three months ago, Allyson was the first one that they had found. She was the last survivor of a refugee camp somewhere north of here. Her features, while gaunt, were still pretty. She had yet to fully recover from malnutrition but was coming along quite well. As to how she survived so long alone in the camp was something she preferred not to talk about. Noam, on the other hand, had showed up under his own power more recently, still clad in Novian combat armor. Though Frank and Mikey hailed from the Earth Union, they let him hang around. Supposedly he'd become separated from his unit some time ago and had been wandering the woods ever since. The specifics on how that happened remained unclear, however. Noam talked even less than Allyson did and merely getting his name had been a monumental challenge.

Elias was the most recent addition. At the beginning of the war, he had also found himself in one of the refugee camps outside the cities. About six months in he elected to jump ship, grabbing as much in the way of supplies as he could and making a run for it into the wild. Luckily for him, he stumbled across someone's empty vacation home out in the middle of nowhere, where he lived in relative comfort for nearly three years, only venturing out when he had to and talking his way out of any trouble that arrived. Within the last year, however, he'd run out of food and began to starve. In the last few weeks, when it seemed that death was imminent, through pure luck Mikey had stumbled across him in the woods West of the dry docks and brought him here.

Elias pulled his gloves off as he sat down on a folding chair next to the fire. Looking over the flames he watched as Mikey gleefully tore open another Meal Ready to Eat and began chewing on its contents. "Geeze dude. It almost looks like you enjoy those things!"

Mikey looked up, his mouth still full of food. "Better than those worms you were trying to dig out of the mud."

"Fucking Christ! You're lucky to have not contracted face rot." Frank began to chuckle, tapping the tip of his cane on the concrete.

"I still can't believe that you were trying to eat those things," commented Allyson.

"Hey, I'm still alive ain't I?" answered Elias with a wry smile.

Allyson rolled her eyes. She then reached into her bag, pulling out an olive drab wool blanket which she proceeded to wrap herself in. "It is so cold here. I can't wait for spring."

"Maybe if you ate more, get a nice layer of fat to keep you warm, like us." Elias grinned facetiously.

"One bite of those things and I'm full." Allyson gestured through the blanket at the pile of MRE wrappers around Mikey's feet.

106

"Whatever you don't eat," Mikey swallowed, "I'm happy to finish." He threw down another wrapper.

Elias turned left, facing Noam. "So, Noam, what you like to eat?" He punched Noam's shoulder.

Noam didn't seem to notice, merely continuing to stare at the flames, dull eyed.

"Well fuck you too Noam!" Elias waved his hands in dramatic fashion. Again, Noam didn't react. "Just kidding Noam, you know we love you."

Noam blinked.

"Ha ha! See, he loves us too!" exclaimed Elias. To this, Allyson just rolled her eyes again.

"You know, I bet Noam could take you out one handed," said Frank, looking over at Elias, smiling.

"I bet he could Frank, I bet he could."

Noam remained still, unwavering.

"'Aight, yeah…" Elias rubbed his hands together before warming them closer to the fire. An awkward silence ensued.

…

Eventually, Allyson spoke up. "So, when are we going to get off this planet?"

"You know how to fly a ship?" Mikey looked over at her.

"No…" She sank deeper into her blanket. "How'd that antenna work out for you? That one you found a few days ago?"

"Antenna's fine. It's the radio system connected to it that's toast. The previous owner gutted the thing."

Elias grimaced. It would have been nice reaching someone and finding a way off this world. "I still say that we should take one of the trucks for a ride, see if there is anyone around the cities North or West of here."

"Elias…"

"I mean, we've got those bedsheets to use as white flags, so we shouldn't have to worry *too much* about getting shot at, if there's even one soldier left on this planet." Elias looked over at Noam. "Sorry, not talkin' about you, Noam."

"Elias, it's not that. I'd rather wait 'till it's warmer. If the truck breaks down in the middle of nowhere, I'm in no mood to freeze to death overnight. Furthermore, the road North has washed out, and the bridges west of here are destroyed. Anyway, we've got time." Mikey gestured towards a supply crate just outside their circle.

"Yeah, but I'll admit flat out, I'm getting bored."

"Enjoy the weather. Keep scavenging. It's a beautiful time of year," answered Mikey.

Elias then looked over at Allyson. "You know, *we* could always do something fun."

"Bite me."

"My thoughts exactly."

At this Frank burst out laughing, which soon gave way to drawn out coughs. Eventually he recovered, wiping his face with his burn scarred hand. "You know, you're not as charming as you think you are."

"Aren't I?"

"No, you're not."

"Aren't I though?"

Mikey then tapped Frank on the shoulder. "You really think you're going to talk sense into this kid?"

"Noam knows what I'm talking about, am I right Noam?" Elias slapped Noam's back, causing him to rock forward slightly.

Noam blinked.

"You see, screw you guys, I've got Noam!" Elias started to sing, "Noam is the best!"

"I can't tell if he's going to kill you in your sleep, or maybe let you live for a few more days," said Frank.

"Eh, don't worry about it. We all love you Elias," joked Allyson.

"Love you too."

"God, why do I bother?" Allyson looked up into the darkening sky shaking with laughter.

The sky had since changed from a shining gold to a darkening purple, though it still retained the occasional orange streak at the lowest levels of the cloud layer. The wind could now be heard blowing around the top edges of the dry dock. Though the breeze had picked up, the three towering walls were positioned in just such a way that the wind did not enter from the open side facing the sea.

Elias reached down into his duffel, pulling out a blanket of his own as well as one of the candy bars that he had found. Pulling back the wrapper he bit into it, savoring the caramel. On this world caramel was expensive, and for the most part a rare luxury. It was amazing what the armed forces brought with them everywhere they went.

"Wait, where did you get that?" Mikey stared at Elias's candy bar, puppy eyed.

"It's a secret." Elias smiled at Mikey as he chewed. "No dude, I'm kidding." He then reached into his duffel and pulled out another one, which he threw to Mikey. He then turned to face Allyson. "Want one?"

"No, thank you."

"What're you on a diet?" Elias tossed one to her and it landed in her lap. "C'mon, get fat like Noam and I here!" At this, she blushed and removed her arms from her blanket to begin unwrapping the treat.

"Yo, Noam! Yo." This time Noam looked over at Elias. "Take this quickly!"

Noam reached out with one gloved hand, gingerly took a candy bar from Elias and put it in one of the pockets of his jacket.

"I bet Noam will be set for a week with that, eh Frank?"

Frank had since slumped forward and was beginning to snore. Mikey proceeded to push Frank back up to a sitting position, waking him up.

"Oh, what?"

"You said you wanted to stay up tonight," answered Mikey.

"Oh yeah." Frank yawned. "I miss being young."

"So, how old are you?" asked Elias. Mikey scowled at Elias, but Frank didn't seem to care.

"82, young one."

"And what are you doing on this God forsaken planet? Nearly everyone else I met prior to the war here were eggheads. You don't seem to be one of them."

"Well, believe it or not I was actually kind of important until a few years ago."

Elias looked at him questioningly.

"I'll tell you that, later," said Frank, eyeing Noam.

"So, you're really going to leave me in suspense?" asked Elias.

"I suppose so." Frank smiled.

Elias sighed, then turned back to Mikey. "You wanna go looking for more people tomorrow? Expand our ever-growing empire here at the dry dock?"

"Not worth trying, I've been through every area within 5 kilometers of this place. Everyone has left."

"More so died than left," added Allyson.

Mikey leaned back in his chair, finishing off the candy bar and throwing its wrapper aside. "Help me search for radio parts tomorrow."

"Sure," answered Elias.

"The civilian network is down as far as I can tell, but I'm hoping that there is enough of the old military or scientific network still up for us to reach Burk or New Bideford. If there is anyone else left on this planet, they'd be in those two cities."

"True, true." Elias stared at the campfire for a moment, lost in thought. "Never been to New Bideford."

"Only rubble," an unfamiliar voice stated dryly.

Everyone turned to Noam, the unexpected source of the words. When it became clear that Noam had nothing more to say, Elias turned back to Mikey. "Well, shit."

"Yeah." Mikey rubbed his left temple, wide eyed. "If and when we get a radio up and running, I'll still reach out to New Bideford. But wow."

Frank looked back to Noam. "You sure about that?"

Noam only stared back.

"Well then." Frank leaned back, a disappointed expression across his face.

They sat in silence for a minute, looking up into the now black sky.

"Well, on that note, I think it's about time for me to hit the sack," said Frank.

"You need any help getting into your tent?" asked Mikey.

"No, I should be all set. Thank you." Frank exhaled as he stood up from his chair, leaning heavily on his cane.

"You have a good night!" said Allyson, giving a small wave which Frank returned in kind. He then proceeded to walk towards the back of the dry dock, out of range of the campfire's light.

Noam then also stood up, gave a subtle bow, turned, and walked off into the darkness.

"So, how long you think we're going to be here?" asked Elias.

Mikey eyed Allyson before answering. "I'm hoping that once we get that radio up, we'll be able to reach someone who can send a signal out of atmosphere."

"Wouldn't said 'someone' have already left if they had that capability?"

Mikey looked at Elias with a semi-dead expression. "Let us hope, that for one reason or another, they are still here."

At this, Allyson got up relatively quickly, wishing them both a polite, albeit rushed, goodnight. Once she had left, Mikey spoke up again.

"You know, I was hoping not to upset her."

"Yeah, sorry about that."

Another moment of silence passed.

"So honestly, what's your assessment?"

"We're going to be here for a long time."

Elias let out a low groan, rubbing his temples with his hands. "So, we don't have a ship. Even if we did, we can't fly it," said Elias, leaning back in his chair. "And despite having vehicles, we have no roads on which to drive them."

"And it's too risky trying to drive through the woods, at least right now," said Mikey completing the thought.

"So, what are you thinking?"

"Pretty much what I said earlier. Wait until it's warmer, then I'd like to start using the trucks to venture out further. For now, though, we should seriously consider making preparations for living here. At least for a while."

By now the fire was starting to wind down, its dimming light only barely illuminating Mikey's face. Elias looked up into the blackness of the sky above them. "You think they're still fighting up there?"

"No idea." At this, Mikey stood up slowly, pushing his chair back and re-adjusting his jacket. "If you could make sure the door is shut before you go to sleep?"

"Afraid of ghosts?" teased Elias, attempting a wry smile.

"More so than you might expect." Mikey put on an olive drab cap and stepped the rest of the way out of the fire's light, disappearing into the darkness.

Now only Elias stared into the remnants of the fire, the ashes changing from a crackling yellow to dull orange. Without the flames, the piercing cold of the night could now be felt. Elias shivered. It was time to go to bed. He stood up, and then stepped out into the darkness. A moment later, the fire died.

Purgatory

13 July 2435 – New Bideford, Echelon

She stretched, eyes closed, enjoying the warm light. Laying her head back on the rubber beach chair, she began to nod gently to the beat of the music. It was some sort of reggae tune, and though she could barely understand the words she enjoyed it. Something about peace and living life. She had long black hair with a thin frame, such that her rib cage could be seen. She was also fairly tall, so that lying flat her bony feet hung off the edge of the chair.

Opening her eyes, she looked through round green lenses at the bright heat lamp she had set up to face her, then back up at the yellow umbrella. Steam emanated from the lamp as raindrops attempted to accumulate on it. Though the umbrella did not completely stop the mist, the combination of the two was enough. The song then changed. Recognizing the tune, she began to sing along.

"Have no worries, tout bagay anfòm," she sang along. "When they say there's no more war I say, 'I go home.'"

When she found the radio a few months ago she wasn't expecting it to work, much less there to still be any radio stations broadcasting. The broadcaster clearly loved his tunes and had an impressive selection of them. He never spoke during the broadcasts though, only switching from song to song, somewhat randomly. Whoever it was, it was comforting to think that there was someone else out there.

A few minutes later the song concluded, and she sat up slightly, adjusting the yellow and white striped top of her bikini. Looking left along the rocky shoreline, she stared at the run-aground battleship a quarter mile away. It was a massive thing, with burnt holes in the sides of the hull and lowered guns. Rain ran down its sides washing oil and hydraulic fluids down into the seawater around it. Throughout the sheen of oil, pieces of metal and waterlogged equipment floated in and out with the lapping waves. To the right about the same distance away the burnt-out frame of a boathouse remained. Scattered in between were the wreckages of various boats and landing craft, for the most part reduced to only their metal and plastic components.

Grabbing hold of a bottle of wine she took a swig from it, then holding it up to admire its shape. Whatever it was, it was good. The label had long since faded away, and she primarily identified the type by the shape of the bottle. Tilting it up one more time she finished it off, and threw the bottle spinning into the sea. A few months ago, searching through what was left of the city, she had found the remains of a package store. It had been surprisingly well stocked, and as a result she still had multiple cases of assorted alcohol at her disposal. It would have been nice if she had such luck finding food.

She had been here since the beginning. When it all started, three, maybe four years ago, she had come to this city after the evacuations. It was said that its location had no military value, thus the Novian army had allowed in a substantial number of refugees in from surrounding towns. Early on it was good living, for wartime at least. Crowded, but safe. With her toes she picked up a spent shell casing, spinning it around and then flicking it away. Apparently, someone on the other side didn't get the memo.

She sighed audibly. It'd been a very long time since she'd seen another person, or rather, a live one. She looked over at the pile of skulls a few feet away, her "memorial" for this place. Picking one up in her left hand, she turned it to face her and stared into its empty sockets.

When shit hit the fan, she had made one decision: that she would survive this. While people died in droves around her, freezing to death in the elements, burning to death in the city, or simply starving, she continued on. Having never established a sense of normalcy in life she adapted, adjusted, evolved in a way. She had pried frozen supplies from dead hands and stripped their bodies when she needed clothing. With an unnatural will to live, she had continued forward. Thus, the people had died, the soldiers had left, and the machines ceased to function. Now here she was, the one and only, refusing to die. The only foe she had left to beat was time itself, and even that no longer seemed daunting.

Putting the skull back down, she turned right to look at another bottle of wine a few feet away on the rocks. Reaching out only to find that it was a few inches beyond her grasp, she elected to just leave it. She had time. She had lost track of how long she had been here, on this patch of deserted shoreline. One day faded into the next, and as productive as she attempted to be early on, it never really amounted to anything. She quite literally knew every inch of the city, down to every ruin and pillar. Outside the city was not much more interesting. Throughout the surrounding forests was a plethora of wreckages and blast craters, most anything useful having been either destroyed or taken away already. Ultimately, her searches only confirmed one thing: that she was truly, unquestionably alone.

Hearing what sounded like the beginning of a wind gust, she reached over and turned the radio down. Despite a there being only a slow breeze, the sound continued to grow, slowly escalating into an airy roar. Standing up from her chair, she looked out to sea, eye's squinting at the grey wall of mist. A few minutes later, far out over the water a white object came into view. Finally able to focus on it, she could see its long fuselage and wings, as well as the white vapor trail the craft left behind it. Definitely not military. Stepping forward into the rain, she stared at it uncomprehendingly as it approached.

"Wow," she said aloud. She didn't think this would ever end.

Made in the USA
Middletown, DE
08 April 2021

37212199R00073